CIVIL BLOOD

A Story

BY Steve Nelson
EDITED BY Chris Sanders

PAGE PUBLISHING, INC.
New York, NY

First originally published by Page Publishing, Inc. 2015

ISBN 978-1-68139-450-3 (pbk)
ISBN 978-1-68139-451-0 (digital)

Printed in the United States of America

CHAPTER 1

SWIM HOLE

The day started like any other Tennessee day for the brothers McSweeney, Joe and Jim. Joe, seventeen, had just finished high school; and Jim, eleven months younger and two inches shorter, would graduate next year. JJ, as they were called, were inseparable. Where there was one, the other was soon to follow. People would rarely call them by their own names, and it was always a question if you found one without the other.

This scorching July day would be spent like normal at their favorite fishing hole with some friends. The Hole was a small pond, not much bigger than an acre, and it was tucked away in a clearing between a few small hills just outside of the McSweeney woods. They had a tree swing set up on a dusty Red Maple, and there was a sheer limestone face on one side that the boys would have diving contests on. They spent many hours at the Hole, and today would be business as usual.

By noon, it was an honest ninety degrees, and no clouds in sight. Joe was up on the tree swing, and Jim remarked to their friends that Joe had been more quiet than usual. They told him, "Prob'ly 'cause of the war, he wants to go join the army and fight."

It was 1862, and the war between the states was well into its second year. Jim was surprised to hear this news since him, and Joe usually told each other everything. He wondered why this time was different. Jim shrugged it off and thought he would ask him about it later.

Joe was planning on enlisting next month after his eighteenth birthday. Some of Joe's friends had already gone off to fight, and he figured it was his time to go too. Joe was worried though about what Jim would do. To Jim, there never was a question. If Joe was signing up, he would be with him. Today, the brothers did not let the war interfere. This day would be like all the others—sunburned bodies with a little pond water in their stomachs for good measure.

On the one-mile trek home, Jim popped the question. Joe confirmed their friends' suspicions about going off to fight in the war.

Jim asked, "Is that it, then?"

Joe replied, 'It is, then."

Dried off now, and with their house in view, Joe told Jim not to say anything at supper.

"I'll take care of everything," he told Jim. Jim nodded in agreement. They had a way of communicating without talking. They had spent so much time around each other, they had an uncanny knack of knowing what the other was thinking. Some occasions they rarely spoke at all, just communicated with "the look." Their twenty-year-old sister Alice saw them walking up and hollered, "Supper will be ready in an hour!"

They both gave each other the look and trotted up the path to the front porch.

The McSweeney family did well for themselves. The old man had a forty-acre corn ranch just outside of the city of Selmer. They had a nice three-bedroom house with two stories, not very common in those parts.

There was no shortage of food, and they were close enough to town to have everything a family could possibly need in West Tennessee. There were four siblings, but their oldest sister Annie had already left for college in Memphis. The McSweeneys were very proud of their children. The whole family was well-liked and respected. Even Joe and Jim had managed to earn the respect of the local townspeople, who thought they were much more responsible and mature than their years led them out to be. Old Man McSweeney was tough on his boys, but he was fair. He raised them to be self-reliant and respectful, and they turned out just the same.

At the supper table, things were quieter than usual, and the Old Man had figured out why long ago. He knew Joe was thinking about enlisting in the Confederate Army, but he said nothing because he wanted Joe to be absolutely sure about the decision. As it was, Joe came right out and said it, "I'll be leaving in three weeks to sign up for the South." The Old Man nodded, and Mrs. McSweeney looked down at her dinner plate. This was no surprise, but what was said next was indeed.

Jim blurted out, "I'm going with Joe!"

All was silent for a few seconds as the fear was allowed to settle in and digest. Ms. McSweeney was a strong, stalwart woman, but she allowed the cracks in her armor to show with a single tear that she quickly blotted with her napkin. The Old Man tried the sensible approach. "Jim, don't you want to finish school first?"

Jim just shook his head, and the Old Man could tell that, just the same as any other day, Jim would be by his brother's side no matter what. He took some small comfort in that. "Well, I guess there is no stopping you boys," the Old Man muttered. "You're both almost adults now, you'll have to make your own decisions soon enough." He silently wished the war would end tomorrow, though he knew it was not going to happen.

Many of the Southern states had already seceded from the Union. He had seen the heartbreak of war slash through the hearts of townspeople who had lost loved ones already. He did not approve of the war, nor did he take any sides. He thought these damn politicians should just "work it out," like how the local feuds got solved. He had never owned a slave, but he did not feel like the government should be telling people what they can and can't do, and then there were the Southern thoughts that the war was not about slavery at all, but about Northern tyranny—and he was just not sure about any of it. He was, however, against good people taking up arms against one another and spilling innocent blood on the soil of a great nation. He thought of a conversation he had in town awhile back with a group of men talking about the war, and how one man had made the statement, "A rich man's war and a poor man's fight." It was truer now than it had ever been. How poor he would be without his boys around to brighten the day.

The dinner was finished, and the boys were out doing their evening chores when Joe remarked, "Why didn't you tell me you wanted to go with me?"

Jim just gave him the look and shrugged his shoulders. Joe returned the look, patted him on the shoulders, and said, "What would I do without ya?" They were going. That was it.

Though Joe was happy his brother wanted to go with him, he was a little worried about how Jim would adjust. In a way, it made him feel easier about what was going to happen to him, but now he was spending all his worry on his brother. He thought of how he would be constantly shouldering extra burden just to make his brother feel more comfortable, and he knew he would do it. He knew he would, at a moment's notice, make any amount of sacrifice if it meant his brother would benefit. It was comforting, but at the same time bothersome and just plain confusing all around. For the first time, he considered the possibility of death in the war. Joe hoped he would make it back home—with his brother, of course. The rest of the night was empty and quiet. Not one more word was so much as grumbled about the situation. This night carried on like any other, except Ma and Pa McSweeney had lost a little bit of themselves, and the two heartbeats of their young sons as well.

It would be twenty days before they shipped out. For JJ, it would be a one-hundred-and-twenty-mile hike upstate to a staging area West of Nashville. For the next two weeks, the McSweeney family saw as much of each other as possible. The Old Man went hunting and fishing with the boys as much as he had time for, even letting some of the farm duties slip as he could afford to. The dinners were bountiful, and the breakfasts were almost too much to put down. Pa McSweeney went into town and spent a pretty penny on a nice fat hog and some fine whiskey that was brought over from Kentucky. They played and laughed and sang and drank. Joe and Jim thought little about shipping out during those two weeks, and they felt for a while like they were living a dream, but the reality of their decision was about to come crashing down on them, and too soon, for that matter.

Their waiting days were up, and the time had come to say good-bye. They all boarded a train for Lawrenceburg where the boys would meet up with their new company. The ride was bumpy and coarse; the comforts of train riding had not been considered much before, though it was a sight better than riding in a carriage. The sun was silently peeking through the morning haze, and they all felt the dawning of a new time. Alice silently wished them the best, Ma was just silent, and Pa was trying to be cheerful for the boy's sake. He told some stories about when he was a young lad and there were troubles with some outlaws who used to live nearby the farm. Pa had taken a stand to them and nearly got killed in a brawl where one of the "bad guys" swung an axe and nearly stuck it in his back, if it weren't for some hard leather suspenders he had been wearing. "Almost got myself a brand," he remarked.

Finally, after some hours, the rickety train pulled into Lawrenceburg. The long, exasperating sigh of the engine's steam compartment was all that Ma McSweeney could bear. She began to cry herself out. Pa comforted the boys by putting his burly arms around both of them in one swift but careful move. He said, "Look now, you boys keep a low profile. Don't you go volunteerin' for any old thing, you hear? If there was one thing I taught you, it's to do the right thing, so keep your heads down and your eyes up." Pa looked at his boys one last time. At five feet eleven inches, Joe was a few inches taller than Jim, and Pa thought he had grown five since the train ride.

"'How did they get so damn big just like that?" he wondered aloud.

"Don't you worry, Pa," Jim remarked, "I'll take care of ol' Joe here." Joe was stunned. He gave Jim "the look," which made Jim laugh out loud. They all had one last smile together, and that was it. JJ hugged their mother and off they went.

CHAPTER 2
THE MARCH

Jim, being the younger of the two, was naturally more inquisitive, asking Joe all sorts of questions about what they were to expect. Joe tried to answer some, but most were met with that patented gaze. They got their directions from a Confederate Army steward that had met them at the train station, and they were off walking. After a mile or two, they came to a broken-down old barn, from which they could hear quite a ruckus going on inside. It reminded Jim of school recess, to which Joe replied, "I don't think they are playing blind man's bluff though."

They stepped inside. "Whoa, there must be one hundred people inside here," Joe remarked. They gave each other "the look," only it was different this time. The noise inside was deafening, so it made it much easier for them to avoid any contact.

There were men fifty years old inside, alongside boys younger than Jim. The reek of the place permeated their nostrils. They recognized a few people here and there but said nothing. Like Pa had told them, they kept a low profile. One big surly gent with tattered brown overalls looked down at them and belched a long, drawn-out whiskey-laced "hello there!" Joe just smiled and nodded. They found a small corner where no one was sitting and camped out until they were called for.

All around people were chatting up stories about the war, home, and various other social topics. After sitting there for a few early afternoon hours, a few younger boys came by with some food for everyone. Joe asked curiously what they were being fed. The one taller boy responded, "Salt pork and hard tack, get used to it." The piece of pork they got was bluish in color and had a crust of salt layered all around it. It looked more like something Ma would throw out, rather than serve for lunch. It tasted like salt-covered cardboard, but they were happy to have something. The aptly named "hard tack" was a piece of concrete like bread that had the consistency of gravel, if you had the nerve and the teeth to take a bite of it. Jim doused his in some water, and it made the experience slightly better, but still awful.

Soon after "lunch," a man came by and separated everyone into squads. It turned out that JJ didn't even have to move from their cozy corner, so they were satisfied with that. The boys made little conversation and sat there observant of all the others who were all seemingly exhilarated to go and fight the North. Jim leaned over and asked, "Is this what Dad meant about keeping a low profile?"

Joe just looked at him and stated mildly, "Kind of."

Both boys were glad they were staying the night, the train ride still wearing on them. They were informed they would move out at noon tomorrow. They would all have to be sworn in and then they would be hiking until sundown, where they would make camp and await further instruction. Joe thought about his mother and wondered where she was and what she was doing.

Mr. and Mrs. McSweeney did not say much to each other on the way home, but both felt the weight of this current turn of events. They both already missed their sons terribly, and both wondered how they would be able to cope if one or both of them should not come home. At dinner, she remarked, "What are we to do, Pa?" With a tone that could make a grizzly bear weep. Pa reminded her that there were many, many parents out there going through the exact same thing right now, and that they should be happy their sons were growing up into men. He assured her they would be looked after and cared for, though he was not so sure of that himself. "It's all for the Lord to decide now," he said. And she prayed even harder than she had before.

At 5:00 p.m., the boys were given another piece of salt pork and another "bread rock," as Joe started calling it, though neither McSweeney ate much of either one. "I suppose this stuff will do if you are starving," Jim said, but all Joe could think of was the bacon they had for breakfast that day along with his mother's scrambled eggs, fresh from the coop.

"Hope we get some real food tomorrow," Joe thought out loud.

"Me too," Jim retorted, and with that, both boys started to drift off into the haze that occurs when one has been upturned into a new and unfamiliar environment, unsure of the next moment as if their dreams and nightmares could come true at any moment. They slept well.

The next morning started at 5 a.m. with loud bursting bugle blasts. Both boys had pits in their stomachs, which were making the typical noises associated with such feelings. Their eyes were wandering all over the place, and their nerves were peaked on high alert. *It's the not-knowing*, Joe thought to himself. He hoped his brother felt better, but by the looks of him, he was in the same boat.

Breakfast was served by some local women at six thirty. JJ, being raised on a farm, knew how to tell time without a watch. The eggs were tolerable. "Nothin' like Ma's," Joe remarked, "'biscuits are good though, grits ain't half bad either."

Jim nodded and slurped down his remaining grits. After their bellies were full and they had washed up a bit, instructions were given for the day. They would march until sundown and then make camp, eat, and then the next set of instructions would be given. Joe surmised that they would be making changes here and there concerning where the enemy was, what he was doing, and how the battle was going. *The enemy*, Joe thought to himself. *Who is the enemy anyway?*

Jim noticed some of the other younger boys rubbing their eyes and acting a little more like teenagers than they had seemed yesterday. "Hell, if they can do it, so can we," he said aloud. "Just have to remind myself everybody has got to do it."

Joe caught him talking to himself, but he said nothing at first. He felt the weight of his younger brother come rushing over him like an angry tidal wave and staggered a bit. "Remember, Jim, we stick together, and we will get through this."

Jim gave him "the look" and said, "Nothin' to it but to do it."

Joe was a little stunned. "Where did you hear that?" Joe remarked with a half-chuckle.

"Some guy over there was saying it," replied the younger McSweeney. Joe smiled at his younger brother and told him, "I like that, Jim, that's a good attitude!" Jim smiled back, and the boys got ready to move out.

Just a dozen or so men in the entire company had weapons. They came to find out everyone would get one when they got to Nashville. Joe had a secret. The day before they left, which seemed like weeks now, but was only two days ago, Pa McSweeney had pulled his oldest prodigy aside and gave him something. Before he did so, he said only one thing: "There will come a time when this will hurt you more than it will help you, hopefully you will do the right thing." He unwrapped a palm-sized Derringer pistol and placed it in Joe's hand.

The first day of marching went by quickly, as the boys found out. They were always moving, no time to think. They passed a lot of remarkable things along the way, like several people waving and hollering at them, but nobody said anything. *No time to think, just keep it moving*, Joe thought to himself. Occasionally (very rarely) the company would stop when weapons were offered. The oldest men received the weapons and whatever ammunition they were paired with. It was a mix of old hunting rifles and some handed-down flint-lock pistols. This first day was, at least, not enough to make mince-meat of their legs and feet. They made camp in a small field at the back of someone's farm.

Even at camp, the boys—and pretty much everyone else—had little to say. They could now feel, a little anyway, the crushing weight of their dire situation and for the first time a bit of remorse swept over the company as if it came in with the wind. Joe was the last of the two McSweeney boys to fall asleep, and he looked over at his little brother and thought, *Nothin' to it but to do it*. He closed his eyes and fell asleep with a glimmer of hope in his brain.

The second day of marching started earlier than everybody expected, which was met with many groans and mumbling. They would only stop for chow this time, and they covered over thirty miles. Men started to get sore and complain. Sprained ankles, blisters on the feet, and sore knees were now commonplace. There was no one to look after them with any bandages or ointments, so the grumbling seemed to get louder as they marched. Jim was noticing a lot of the younger boys, and some of the older men looking like they were not going to make it. He never said a word about it, but once in a while, Joe heard him, almost silently, remind himself, "Nothin' to it but to do it." This helped Joe immensely. He thought he would have to carry the burden for two people instead of just himself. Jim was getting along fine though. He never faltered, never complained about anything. At times, Joe thought he was the younger brother, but then he felt his pocket and remembered he had the gun.

Joe thought about what his father told him, and it swam around in his mind for quite a while. He wondered when that time would come when he would have to use it and also wondered when it would become a problem. Joe recalled he told his father that he would make him proud, and he felt better that he would just know, when the time came, what the "right thing to do" was. It helped a lot that Jim seemed to be taking care of himself just fine.

Day 2 passed with relative ease for the McSweeney boys, and day 3 was already coming to an end. Their main concern was the terrible food. Salt-pork and hard tack were taking their toll (or lack thereof) on the McSweeney stomachs. The brazen sun was starting to duck behind the hills, and the sweat filling the men's eye sockets began to wisp away. Everyone's hat was soaked through with the sweat of a day's march. Some of the men had fallen out and were never seen again. If you couldn't make this march, then you would likely not last long in combat. So they were left, and their contracts nullified. Nearing the end, they were quickening their pace to make a certain point the commander had been pushing for, when Joe suddenly stumbled. His right toe caught a root in the ground and spun him forward into the brush. Before he even realized what was happening, his father's Derringer came loose out of his pocket and lay there gleaming in the dust and dirt. He could feel the eyes penetrating his body. Not many people have seen this type of pistol before, and Joe could only imagine what they would do to get it. Joe immediately realized what his father was talking about when he gave Joe the gun and quickly scrambled to reach it. Just as he almost had his hand over it, a tarnished boot stepped on it. Joe looked up. He saw one of the sergeants pursing an evil grin at Joe as he lay there, prone in the dirt.

Joe looked down at the boot, and then up, and to his complete surprise saw the sergeant lurching through the air as if he had just been launched out of a cannon. It was Jim who had hurled himself against the weight of the man. Joe quickly scooped up the pistol and replaced it in his pocket rather matter-of-factly. He put his hand out to help his brother up, with a new light in his eye. The airborne sergeant, and everyone else around now knew that if you messed with one, you would get both. Joe was a little embarrassed, but at the same time gleaming with pride over the actions of his little brother.

Jim was smiling ear-to-ear. "Nothin to it but to do it," he beamed. It didn't take very long for this news to travel through the ranks. The busted-up sergeant hobbled back into formation without a word.

The march ended within the hour. Jim asked Joe about the pistol at chow time. Joe related the whole story and added that the Old Man had given him some money as well. Joe told his little brother to keep silent about it, and he never spoke another word regarding either the pistol or the money. To Joe, this was an awakening. All the time he was watching Jim's back, and then this happened. He should have been watching his own back, confident that his little brother would be there when he needed. Confident that Jim would do what his Pa told him to do—the right thing. Jim fell quickly asleep, and Joe looked over at him and again felt like the older brother. He felt something new this time though. They were partners.

While Jim was sleeping, Joe got some looks, and a few of the other men came by to make idle chitchat. *Amazing what a little weapon will do to people's attitudes*, he thought. The sergeant who had stepped on the pistol even came over. Joe, at first, was fearful, but the man put him at ease right away with his demeanor. Joe woke up his brother, who was startled by the appearance of the sergeant, and jumped up, guns blazing.

"Whoa there," the sergeant said. "I'm not here to cause any further ruckus." He went on to explain that he was trying to shield the sight of the weapon from the other men, and he had no intention of taking it. The boys were calmed by the sergeant's easygoing manner, and they immediately took a liking to him.

His name was O'Brien. He was a twenty-year-old from Pulaski. The boys had been there once on an outing with their father. It was a very similar town to Sumner, and they started talking about farming and back home, enough to make them all a little homesick. O'Brien had seen some pretty bad fighting earlier in the war. He got a battlefield promotion after the Battle of Shiloh and was considered a war hero in some circles. Him and a dozen other men held off a whole company and protected the retreat of around a thousand men. The boys were astonished by this man and his tales. It was clear that O'Brien took an immediate liking to the boys as well. Too many of the soldiers he had come across were maladjusted and uncouth. He was raised the same way that the McSweeney boys were. He took no pleasure in killing, and even on the battlefield, he held his composure and kept his bearings. O'Brien was a true leader, and he had earned every bit of his promotion. He was well-liked around the company and would turn out to be a valuable friend and ally to the boys. The boys, being unaccustomed to army rank and structure, had no idea that O'Brien was the commander of the entire company, and their relationship with him turned more than a few eyes. They had a laugh about Jim's outburst, said goodnight, and went to sleep, a little easier than they had expected—all three.

The company was a little more than halfway to the staging area. A few of the weak, injured, and ill were left behind—and as many were added along the way. "That's how these things go," O'Brien said to the boys as they were marching along. Their total number was close to eighty. The fourth day came and went without incident, only twenty-five more miles to go. They were all getting stronger from the marching and camping, including the McSweeney boys, who put on a little swagger now that they were seasoned marchers. They were also getting anxious, and nervous—something that O'Brien noted and let the boys know would happen, so they were mindful of their own emotions. The manner of everyone around them seemed to be restless, and the boys, though they were feeling just as keyed-up as everyone else, kept their low-profile, as their father had requested.

As they were marching along, O'Brien was telling the boys a few of his fantastic war stories. He also let the boys know once he got to Nashville, he might be leaving the Confederate Army. "No more of this fighting between the states," he said. "I'll be headin' west to open up a business or fight some Indians."

JJ were impressed with O'Brien's travels and stories. Marching with him made it go a little easier, and the time passed quickly. They even managed a smile every now and then. O'Brien was impressed too. He thought the boys were his age, the way they acted, and felt like he had found a couple of real gems. He was reconsidering leaving the army just yet.

CHAPTER 3

NASHVILLE

The company added about twenty men, and now more than half of them had weapons. They would soon be issued some type of uniform, mess kits, boots, and everyone would be given a firearm, with which they would learn how to operate. The weapons the army had were not the best of their time, and they were often difficult to operate and cumbersome. Still, it was better than not having a weapon. The main purpose of a firearm in combat is to wound or maim the enemy, and those weapons needed to be held rather close to the enemy to accomplish such a purpose, which often led to hand-to-hand combat. O'Brien had many horror stories to tell. He had seen limbs and heads ripped from bodies, men lying there with mortal gashes from bayonets, pleading to be killed. Men lying in pools of their own carcass, left alone to die a slow, agonizing death. The boys were listening to these stories from O'Brien, and it made the war all that much more real. They had not seen any fighting yet and were still unsure what to expect.

After spending a few days in the staging area, the men began to get more restless. The company had orders to meet up with the battalion at the Tennessee/ Missouri border twenty-five miles away. The battalion commanding officer was Major Soles. O'Brien (O-B as the McSweeney boys began to call him) had served with this Major Soles before, and he made no attempt to hide his personal disregard for the major. "He waited for things to happen before he would act," O'Brien commented to JJ. "And waiting in war is akin to suicide."

This was another reason O-B wanted out of the Confederate Army. Bad leadership was everywhere in the war and accounted for many lost lives.

On a dark and murky Tennessee morning, the eighty-or-so odd men of this ragtag company moved out for the Missouri border. The weather was unbearably humid, yet there was no rain in sight. They managed only fifteen miles through the rugged, hilly terrain that day. Hopes were that they would make the battalion rendezvous tomorrow. They made camp in a low valley surrounded by hills and woods.

"This will be a nice cool, protected area," Joe said aloud to himself, and O'Brien agreed, happy he had chosen a good area for camp. The hills went for a mile in every direction, and without the moon that night, it would have been impossible to see your hand in front of your face. They were cut off from the world, by trade and now by sight. The only things that could see them were the god-awful mosquitoes, which were relentless as usual. Fires were started quickly.

Everyone in the company had had their fill of the day's marching. Most of the men were drenched from head to toe, stinking loudly in the dark. From the camp, a few posts were put up halfway up the hills, to give warning in case they were ambushed. The boys were lucky and did not draw watch that night. The men all stripped down to their skivvies, lit their smokes and pipes, and got ready for chow. There was an air of excitement sweeping through the company. They were soon to meet the enemy, and they all knew it.

"This is what everyone joins for," O'Brien stated, with the tiniest bit of sarcasm in his voice. Right around seven o'clock, a little breeze swept down from the hills and knocked about fifteen degrees off the temperature. The men all sighed with whatever happiness they could muster. By eight, everyone was ready to bed down and thought little of doing it all over again the next day.

The bugle sounded at 5 a.m. By seven thirty, they were packed up and mounting the mile-long slopes. JJ were slowly plodding up the harsh terrain next to O-B somewhere near the middle of the pack. The branches and twigs felt like metal spikes on their feet, and every rock was like a knife in the boot. They were cursing the geography of their own home state the entire time up the hill, and then they could see the top of it in the near distance. JJ felt a wave of relief wash over them as they could finally see something other than the blasted hill and the men's boots in front of them. About eighty yards from the top, they felt something they had not encountered before. A sense of uneasiness crept into Joe's heart, and he felt it tugging on his soul. He looked over at O'Brien and could tell he felt the same thing—and then . . .

Gunfire.

It erupted like a snarling pack of rabid wolfhounds. All around them, the boys could feel the shock wave of gunpowder bursts being hurled in their direction. Men started to fall and scream. The Union soldiers immediately flanked the rebel column. Men were dropping on the left, on the right, in front and in back of them. One all-too-long gape at the carnage was all it took for Joe. He grabbed Jim and hit the ground hard. In what seemed like an eternity, but what actually took all of two minutes, the Union Army ambush had rendered this company helpless.

The men of the Union ambush had been stalking the company for a few days, the scouts being able to observe them without being detected. They knew they would have the rebels at an extreme disadvantage on their way up that hill. It was a perfect opportunity with the rebels thinking of nothing but getting over the top of that blasted hill, and with no weapons at the ready, no forward observers, and with the advantage of high ground. It was almost too easy. The rebels walked right into the bloody mess without quarter.

Many of the men who were hit were screaming. Everyone else was as silent as could be. Joe picked up his head and looked around. He saw a few men motionless, some being tended to, some not. Union soldiers started to make their way around the company, grabbing up the rifles and whatever other weapons that were in plain sight. O'Brien leaned over and whispered to the boys, "Just do as they say, nothing sudden, and stay spread eagle on the ground."

The sounds started to become unbearable, with men moaning and screaming, pleading for their lives. Blood started to trickle down the hill where the boys were lying. The crimson river pooled up a little around Joe's boot and made its heartbreaking swirl near the toe before it continued on into the conscience of the other soon-to-be prisoners of war.

The front ten men had literally been cut in half by the initial ambush. After that, there were another twenty or so casualties, of whom seven had met their fate. The rest would soon meet theirs. The stench of men's guts ripped apart filled the air with foulness that could not be spoken of. The wind was rushing down the hill, and everyone got a little sicker, including the Union soldiers. Joe's thoughts turned to his brother, and he looked over at Jim, who was looking back. "I thought I was shot," Jim whispered. Blood was spilled over everything in sight. Death was everywhere.

JJ were grabbed by the backs of their blouses and hurled into a circle of prisoners. They could see the remains of the twenty-some rebels lying on the side of the hill. O-B asked the boys if they were all right. They thought so, but both were still in a state of shock. The Union Army then moved all of the able prisoners to the other side of the hill and did not carry the wounded. The soldiers would not allow the prisoners to witness what happened next. Every ten or twenty seconds, a gunshot would go off. The boys knew what was happening and did not expect it. It seemed to last forever, but in reality took only a few minutes. The moaning had finally stopped. The boys looked around their circle, but nobody looked familiar except for O-B. There the boys sat with their heads between their knees, not knowing what to do or think. Their fates were uncertain.

Finally a Union soldier hoisted them all to their feet and told them to follow him. The soldiers took their prisoners away from the site of the massacre, and they were actually a little relieved. JJ's bodies stopped shaking, and they began to recognize some of the other men who were being led away with them. O-B was standing, talking to one of the Union men.

Since there were no rank indicators, the Union soldiers had no idea that O-B was the head sergeant. They probably figured he was a lowly corporal or something. The air began to return to the boys' lungs. Life was not quite over.

O-B caught up with them and asked the boys again if they were okay. He had witnessed far worse atrocities and told the boys, "You have to wipe it clear and move on, that's the only way to get through it."

The boys asked him what happened. O-B told them that his sergeant in front had not sent any scouts out, and that the rebels had been stalked. "We didn't have a chance, what with our lack of weapons and any real training." O-B went on to tell them that the sergeant was one of the first to be cut down, and his mistake was paid for in full. The boys were still having trouble processing what had just happened, but there would be no time to dwell on it.

They both turned into men right in front of each other that day. Joe was still in shock, but somehow felt proud that they had survived. He turned to look at his brother and noticed a small patch of blood near Jim's lower belly. There was not much blood, but Joe quickly pointed out the stain, and Jim patted it—and to his surprise, he suddenly figured out he had been shot. There was a small fragment lodged in his gut. He was so in shock from the events that happened he didn't even notice. What actually happened was a bullet that had missed its target had hit a rock and splintered right in front of the boys. One of the fragments sprayed upward and into Jim's stomach, right as they had gotten the idea to jump to the ground. The wound itself was slight, but there was a good size chunk of lead lodged in Jim's belly, and it would become a problem if they didn't do something about it.

Joe quickly told O-B, and they washed out most of the blood with some canteen water and quickly bandaged Jim up so he would not bleed through. "It doesn't look so bad, but keep an eye on it, Joe," O-B stated in haste.

Joe told Jim he would fix him up as soon as he could, and Jim said he would keep it to himself and that he was all right. "Don't worry too much about it, Joe, I'll be fine," he said, though he wasn't all that sure about it. Witnessing those executions was enough to keep them from letting on about Jim's wounds. Their captors were not likely to offer any mercy.

Of the eighty men that the company started out with, fifty-eight were left. Only a few were allowed to travel with minor flesh wounds, anyone who was immobilized was shot, thrown into a ditch, and set on fire. Jim may have been one of those rebels, had his wounds been more severe. As far as Joe and O-B could tell, Jim was doing okay, despite having eaten some lead. Only time would tell if he would make it through. The Union soldiers did not waste much more time. The rebels were all informed they would be heading north to Illinois.

"Camp Douglas," O-B replied. None of the rebels knew where they were heading except him, and he was not leading on about it. The stories O'Brien had heard about Douglas were not good stories, and he hoped they were tall tales rather than facts, but he had heard enough to make him worried.

The rest of the rebel soldiers only hoped it was not too far.

After a few minutes of idle chatter and some planning, the prisoners and their captors were off. Joe was concerned about his little brother, though there was little any of them could do. Occasionally O'Brien would check on Jim. He tried to comfort Joe by telling him the wound was not causing any bleeding and that Jim would be fine if he kept pressure on it. Joe could tell that Jim was in some pain though. Some of the other rebels who had superficial wounds were hurting much more, as they could tell, but that did not make their situation any less concerning. Jim vowed to deal with it in his own way, and they kept their mouths shut.

The first few days, everything was basically silent. They marched and camped and ate what little they had. Nobody wanted to speak, Union or Confederate. Though they were enemies, the soldiers from either side felt a kinship of common servitude, and there was little hatred spread around. Near the end of the fourth day, they reached a train station somewhere in Kentucky and were all herded onto a freight train much like cattle would have been. In fact, Joe figured out that they were, in fact, riding in a cattle car. Maybe the Confederates had a sense of humor after all. There was little to no food to go around. Joe and O-B gave everything they could get their hands on to Jim. He was starting to weaken a little from the pain, and his wound was starting to show. He was strong and young, but Joe wondered if that was going to be enough to keep him alive.

Joe had bribed one of the guards to get his brother some medical attention. He soon found out just about anything could be bought, if you had the cash. He still had a decent amount of money from what his father had given him, and he hid it well, showing only what he was intending to bribe with. The soldier he bribed was actually a medic, and he had no problem sterilizing Jim's wound and giving him a few bandages. Jim felt a slight bit better afterwards, and his spirits picked up a little bit. After three days of riding the rails, they arrived in Chicago.

Camp Douglas was mainly a transport camp, since Chicago was the largest railroad hub in the United States and nearly everything passed through there one way or another. With all the wounded and the sheer number of prisoners coming through, it would soon become one of the largest POW camps of the Civil War, and without a doubt the most wretched in the North. The prisoners disembarked and were led off to march the few miles to their new home.

The camp was like nothing the boys had ever seen nor ever heard about. On the outside it looked like any normal army base, like those they had seen pictures and paintings of. The great wooden fences were high and intimidating. The buildings were boxy and rigid. It sat on eighty acres of Chicago flatland and was a large enough space to accommodate thousands of prisoners, which it eventually did. They boys walked under the great archway that was the main gate, and Joe posed the question aloud to himself, "How the heck are we gonna get out of here?"

O'Brien gave him a solemn look and said, "Let's just hope we can make it to tomorrow." Once they got inside, it was apparent that this was no ordinary camp.

They walked in among over a thousand prisoners standing around watching the newcomers arrive like it was some sort of spectacle. The stench of rotting corpses and human waste permeated their nostrils immediately and without warning. Joe looked over at the crowd gathering and noticed nearly all of them were underweight and looked as if they had not had food for days. Some of the men were so gaunt you could see their bones peeking through their skin as if their flesh was hanging on for dear life. The clothes they had on were ratty at best, and only some of them still had shoes. Joe could sense the disease and pestilence by how the men were scratching and picking at themselves. He wondered how many had died from these intolerable conditions. He wondered if his brother would be one of them.

The garrison officer at Camp Douglas at the time was Col. Charles V. DeLand. The colonel was a decent man to be in charge, but he was once a Confederate POW himself and knew all too well what the treatment of prisoners was like in the South, himself being garrisoned at Andersonville, which eventually Camp Douglas would rival in poor treatment of prisoners. His initial attempts at creating tolerable conditions for the prisoners were met with disregard and ignorance, which caused him much frustration throughout the course of his tenure as GO. The frustration resulted in a general sense of carelessness and disdain on the colonel's part. As the boys were walking to their squad hut, they noticed a peculiar-looking device perched just outside of Colonel DeLand's barracks.

It was a creature like construction. There was a spine and limbs. It looked much like a saw horse with ribs sticking out of its center mast. They stopped to take a closer look, and just as they did, O-B grabbed them and hurried them along. "Don't you be messin' around near that thing," O'Brien quipped. "They call that Morgan's Mule, and I hear it's a two-hour ride on its back if you're caught anywhere near it."

As they passed it, Joe and Jim began to realize what the thing was; it was an instrument of torture. Near thirty feet long from end to end, its spine was a plank four inches wide by eight inches thick, and the top was planed off to a sharp edge all the way down its center. The "ribs" were made of planks slightly less in stature but were numerous and arranged to be useful for the same purpose—to be ridden. Ridden by a pack of undeserved and unlucky dogs whose lives were naught cared for. There was a vague smell of turpentine and resin in the air, a likely added discomfort for the unlucky few.

The camp itself was not made to hold prisoners for long periods. It was originally intended to be a holding camp right after the Union Army abandoned it for training purposes. The influx of prisoners was beyond what they had anticipated, and the logistics they had in place could scarcely provide the camp's needs. Things were constantly being cut out of the daily allowances. Disease was rampant, as they soon found out.

Prisoners were dying at an alarming rate, some from lack of nutrition, some from illness, some from the wounds they had suffered prior to their stay at Camp Douglas. The newly arrived men were not used to the blistering cold, and it took some time getting used to. Men were doubling and even tripling up in the bunks, just to get more heat. The prisoners ate whatever they could find—including bugs, rodents, and even stray dogs that would wander into the camp.

It was mid-September and the cold was starting to penetrate through the loosely crafted barracks. They were elevated off of the ground to keep the running rain water and snow from creating vast puddles inside the barracks, but since there were so many escape attempts due to tunnels being dug, the wooden floors had been ripped out and dirt was thrown in until the floor joists were covered. This was cause for much of the disease that was running rampant throughout the camp. They were given rations of beef and bread, though the portions for each barracks were not much to speak of. Every day when the kitchen guards would open the "crumb hole" as they called it, the men would all clamor for it like they were giving out gold. There were two heat stoves found in each barracks, however the misuse of them had long since negated the rationing of coal for their operation.

Fights often broke out for blankets and clothes, none of which resulted in a "winner."

Horror stories were starting to circulate among the newcomers. Men were found dead every morning from frostbite, starvation, and even scurvy. The treatment of the prisoners was abhorrent at best. Men were hung by their thumbs until they snapped or forced to "ride the mule" with weighted legs until something broke, whether it be an ankle, a hip, or a knee. These injuries became permanent, with the unlucky subjects being denied medical attention. If you rode the Mule, you would likely die, unless you had some money or something to bribe the guards with. It was no secret that most of the guards would take any sort of bribe. If you had Federal money on you, well, you could probably escape without anyone knowing. This was another great source of frustration for Colonel DeLand, but for Joe it was a way out, and he had a plan.

Jim had been placed in the infirmary with a small bribe from Joe. He felt a bit of pressure release when Jim was taken away, knowing that, at the least, the bribed guards would take care of him, if anything to get some more money out of it. He was able to check on Jim every now and then, and he seemed to be doing okay, with the limited attention he was getting. O-B made a stop every now and then and was always able to smuggle something interesting for him, like a deck of cards or a piece of cheese. Joe felt it was only a matter of time before the guards, or maybe even some desperate prisoner, would try to extort all of his money, but he had to wait until Jim was rested enough to make a journey.

Two months passed like time was rushing over a waterfall. Joe spent his days playing cards and chatting with O'Brien about what they would do once they got out and where they might go. Joe suggested they visit his uncle in Wisconsin. O'Brien was a little reluctant to be going farther up North, but this was fairly close in a town called Kenosha which was only a few miles from Chicago. The conversation was plenty to keep their minds off the worsening conditions and the death that was all around them. They made the best of what they could though. Between Joe's money and O'Brien's influence, they were able to live at least mildly comfortable. Both men were hungry to no end, and O-B might have killed someone for a sip or two of whiskey.

By mid-January, the cold was claiming three or four victims a day. Those who were weak and frail from wounds did not last very long at all. O'Brien was on water detail one day, and he overheard some guards talking about Joe. They were planning on hanging him by his thumbs to get whatever money he might have. This was all the impetus Joe needed to commence the breakout. "It's time," he said coldly to O-B as they were finishing up the evening's rations. All they needed was a distraction.

The next night was intolerably cold, and a few men in the barracks next to Joe and O-B started a fire in the barracks with some old blocking tinder and a few tree branches they had saved up. With the wind blowing in gusts at around thirty-five miles per hour, it did not take long for the fire to spread. The unwitting southerners had built the fire too close to the doorway, and once the fire was big enough, one big gust took the fire right into the bunk area—and from there it was madness. It was a fortunate thing for Joe and O-B as the barracks that started on fire was right next to the infirmary. Jim was soon shuffled out into the freezing cold to escape the raging inferno. He was not looking well; his face had turned quite pale and was gaunt from lack of nutrition. Joe spotted him immediately and hurried over to where he was standing with O-B in tow.

Some of the guards took to being impromptu firemen right away, but most of them just stood around and watched the stumbling bodies and blistering fires. Joe gave Jim and O-B the patented

McSweeney "look," and they all knew it was time to go. O-B and Joe made themselves look busy helping the guards round up the prisoners from the infirmary and get them to safety, and while they did so, Joe approached one of the guards he knew well. It was the same guard who had taken his money to get Jim into the infirmary. His name was Ford, and he was a tall, lanky fellow with a full beard and a huge scar down the left side of his face, which was a gift to him from the battle of Franklin just a short time ago. He had spent time in this same infirmary, though his care far exceeded that of the prisoners.

Joe slunk close to him. "Ford," he said calmly and under earshot, "we got a request."

Ford looked at him and seemed to know what he was implying. "I knew your pockets was deep, what you got for me?" Ford stated rather matter-of-factly.

Joe showed him over forty dollars in Federal money, which was less than one-third of all the money he had. "Come on with it," Ford stated eagerly.

"You gotta get us out of here right now," Joe said coolly.

O-B rose up and cornered Ford in between the two of them. Ford looked around quickly, noticed the chaos, as well as the fire was still spreading. "Let's go, follow me," he said.

Joe and O-B grabbed Jim and hurried off around the back of the barracks after the lumbering guard. The fence-line guards were all in disarray trying to sort out the confusion. Most of them had left their posts, and it was basically pitch black where the fire was not burning, so the caravan of escapees did not have a problem making it to the front gate. When they got there, things were a different story.

Ford pulled up short of the gate and gave the motion to stop to the boys and O-B. He walked over to the two guards at the gate and started mumbling something to them. After a minute or two, he motioned for them to come closer. Joe approached cautiously with O-B taking up the rear. As they got close, they could see something was amiss. The guard at the gate was trying to bargain for some bribery of his own. "If they ain't got no more money, then you give me some more," they overheard the gate guard say.

Ford replied, "I gave you your share already, now go on and open the gate."

The gate guard turned and looked at Joe. "You ain't getting through here 'til you give me what you got, you little Sunday Soldier."

Joe took a step forward. "I'm sorry, sir. I gave Ford every last dollar I had," he said as he reached in his pocket. The gate guard was visibly upset, and he threw his weapon over his shoulder and reached out for Joe's blouse, but before he could, there was a cold piece of steel shoved directly into his neck.

The guard backed up and saw a shiny silver cap-and-ball Derringer pointed at his face. Neither O-B nor Jim had any idea how Joe managed to keep that pistol from getting confiscated, but it was obvious he went to great lengths to hide it. Ford and the gate guard stood there, jaw dropped and motionless. Quietly and quickly, the boys and O-B moved closer toward the gate and motioned for the guard to open it. O-B grabbed the rifle from the guard and saw that it was not loaded. "This will probably not come in handy," he quipped and tossed the rifle over the gate into the darkness. Once the gate was open, they all made a mad dash for the trees nearby.

As they were running to the trees, Joe could hear O-B chuckling. Jim was still having a hard time moving quickly, so Joe grabbed him by the waist and urged him along. They got to the tree line and ducked behind a large bush. "What the heck are you laughing at?" Joe asked with a half smile on his face.

O-B looked at him, his face still red from the hustle and laughing. "I thought that guard was gonna soil himself," he said. "You sure put a number on him with that little pea shooter, how the heck did you manage to hide that thing?"

All three men had time for a quick laugh, and then something startled them.

One of the barracks had collapsed and sent embers and flame billowing up as far as the eye could see.

They sat for a minute and watched as the flames peeked out over the top of the sturdy wooden fence. They heard the voices of guards clamoring, trying to maintain order. All at once, they were relieved for themselves, having escaped that horrible place and also sad for their comrades, knowing there was a good chance that a lot of those prisoners would never leave it. They stared at the prison camp on fire for more than a few minutes, trying to contemplate their future, their past, and everything in between. Finally O-B perked up and said,

"Well, we best be gettin' a move on. We need to find a place to settle in for the night."

Just as he finished his sentence, they heard a rustling in the bushes nearby. They all crouched down and waited. After what seemed like an hour, but was really a matter of a few minutes, a man appeared to the north of them, silhouetted by the light of the fire. He was walking rather quickly toward them. Joe grabbed on to the butt of the Derringer and clenched it tight in his hand. The man appeared to be hobbling a little, and as he got within about fifteen meters, they could see it was one of the prisoners, a Georgian named Gerald Kinney.

"Hey over here," Joe creaked, making sure not to throw his voice.

Kinney stopped dead in his tracks and looked past them. "Who the heck is that?"

Joe stood up. "It's the McSweeney boys and O'Brien. Over here, Kinney."

He saw them and darted over to where they were. "Damn good to see some friendly faces out here."

O-B looked at him quizzically and said, "How the heck did you get out of there?"

Kinney shuddered a bit and said, "Well, them guards that's normally on the parapet came down to help out with the fire, and I just ran up the ladder and jumped clean over the fence when I thought no one was lookin'."

The boys all chuckled with delight.

"I was like a swan for a minute, gliding through the air as graceful as can be," Kinney said with a little smirk on his face. "I hit the ground pretty hard though, might have messed up my ankle. So where y'all headed?" he asked.

O-B said, "We haven't figured out a place to stay for the night, but we are headed north to Wisconsin as soon as we can, JJ's got some relatives there and maybe some jobs for us."

"Well, follow me, boys," Kinney said with a big grin "I know a Southern sympathizer that lives just around the way. He's an old friend of my pop that moved up here only a few years ago, lucky for us." Kinney started out toward the west end of the tree line.

The boys and O-B took one last look at Camp Douglas in all of its current disarray and were thankful they would have to look upon it no more.

The fire raged all through the night and into the morning. After making some futile attempts to put the fires out, the guards decided it would be best to just let it burn, which actually turned out to be a blessing. The fire had actually cured the area of any disease and rodent problems. When all was said and done, four buildings had burned to the ground, and six prisoners had died—five of smoke inhalation and one was shot trying to escape. A total of twenty prisoners had escaped from Camp Douglas, seventeen of them for good. Over the course of its operation as a Confederate prison camp from 1862 to 1865, Camp Douglas killed 4,524 men; however, there are at least 1,500 soldiers "unaccounted for." The death rate for prisoners at the camp was between 17 and 23 percent. The McSweeney boys, O'Brien, and Gerald Kinney were not among the unfortunate.

All four escapees made it to the sympathizer's house after a good two hours walk through the essentially flat landscape of the Chicago area. Kinney had good navigational skills and had been given excellent directions in a letter from his father. The sympathizer's name was Nelson Donner, and he owned a cattle farm just west of the Chicago area. It was a vast stretch of land, and there was no dwelling in any direction for them to see. Though they had startled the household a bit upon their arrival, they were welcomed by the Donner' family, even at that hour of the night, and immediately Jim was taken in by Mrs. Donner for treatment on his wound. Nelson was a happy, cheerful man—something they had not seen in a long, long time.

The farm was entirely too comfortable for what the trio had previously been accustomed to. They were served a steaming hot beef stew that Mrs. Donner was famous for, and they relished every last bit of it. They were given new clothes, and there were soft hay beds for them to sleep on with linen blankets. Mr. Donner was quite skilled at crafting beer, and all four former prisoners had their fair share of it and traded stories with the Donner family until long after the rooster crowed. The Donners were fascinated and abhorred by the stories of Camp Douglas. They could not believe such a place even existed. They told all the tales of Morgan's Mule and the thumb hangings much to the shock of Mrs. Donner, who at one point had to remove herself from the room. Sleep was soon welcomed and lasted well into the evening, and not one of them woke before lunch. O-B actually slept well into dinnertime, though he was awakened by the luxurious smell of Mrs. Douglas's famous stew and a swift kick from Jim, who was tired of all his slacking off and told him so.

The boys and O-B stayed at the Donner house for another three days. Their bellies were full and morale was high. They stoked fires long into the night, and Mr. Donner was more than generous with his home-brewed beer, which they were happy to take a share of. JJ and O-B had talked quite a bit about their immediate future, and they were all agreed that they should head north to Wisconsin to make the acquaintance of their mother's brother in Kenosha. They had decided they were through with war, especially O-B, who was more than happy to follow the McSweeney boys wherever they were headed. The idea of being out on their own and making a life for themselves was a common topic of conversation, and they were like sponges with ideas, soaking them up and wringing them out with urgency. There was a lot of talk of having their own inn and showing some Northerners a bit of Southern hospitality.

Mr. Donner offered them a map of the area they were going to traverse and pointed out the spots they should avoid. They decided to take most of the journey on at night, at least the first few legs anyway, so they might have a better chance of getting out of the immediate area without being spotted by any Union soldiers. Jim was feeling much better after the last few days of rest, and his pale, gaunt look was starting to disappear in favor of some rosy color. His smile had returned.

They ate breakfast the next morning and prepared to shove off after sundown. They packed up whatever they had into two knap-sacks. Mrs. Donner let them take some nice linen blankets, and they fashioned a few bedrolls out of some old linens and some yarn and stuffed them with soft hay. They took some fresh bread and fruit and each were given a leather cask to fill with water. Kinney was going to stay with the Donners and work on the farm until things blew over with the war. Mr. Donner was happy to have a hand around the farm. Jim, above the others, was truly indebted to the Donners for their hospitality and kindness. He was like a new man, once again ready to take on the world. O-B asked him if he was ready to go, and he replied, "Nothin' to it but to do it!"

Joe smiled.

They bade farewell to the Donners and Kinney around 6:00p.m. There were many things to say in parting, and they all promised to return for a visit one day, knowing full well that there was a good chance it would never happen. Still, it was always a fond memory in the backs of their minds, and it would be a long, long time before any of them forgot what Mrs. Donner's beef stew tasted like. They hesitantly packed up their things and took to the road, feeling anxious to get to Wisconsin and possibly a fresh start.

They walked for many miles before they decided to camp, just before daybreak. The pale morning sky beckoned them to rest, and they were more than happy to oblige. The bright sun made it hard for them to stay asleep, and they did not get much rest, considering they were exhausted from the night's march. Around noon, they were all awake, and they made a fire to warm up and cook a lunch.

"So here we are, just three fellas trying to make it in the world," Joe said with a grin.

Jim gave him "the look," and O-B smiled back with the kind of confidence that only young men have; young men who are on the verge of starting their own life. "Yup, so what do you think we'll call our place?" O-B asked.

Joe replied, "I don't know yet, but it should be something that fits us proper."

Jim chimed in immediately, "Yeah something like Confederate Rejects."

Joe looked over at his brother and let out a loud chuckle for two reasons. He was laughing at the joke, but was also relived to see his brother in good spirits, something he had not seen in a long time.

Joe still had a bit of money left, over one hundred and fifty dollars. They hoped their uncle would have some insight into starting a business and getting them off on a good start. They knew little of Uncle Steve, only what their mother had told them. She mentioned once that he was "a man who knew how to get things done." For the boys in their current situation, this was encouraging. Though there were never many stories about what he was like, they remembered a conversation that they heard between their mother and father regarding Uncle Steve. Mrs. McSweeney received a letter from Uncle Steve in which he asked if the family wanted to join him in Wisconsin on a business venture. The boys overheard their father say, "We don't need any of that money—that's bad money and it will ruin us." At the time, they wondered what "bad money" was, but they seemed to understand a little better as they got older. Uncle Steve was a man who might bend a few laws to "get things done."

CHAPTER 4

UNCLE STEVE

They made the rest of the journey to Kenosha without any hitches or missteps. Wisconsin seemed to be a little less touchy when it came to the war, like it was in another universe, separate from all of the foul talk and bloodshed. They met a few former Camp Douglas prisoners along the way that asked if they could tag along to Wisconsin, so when they finally arrived in Kenosha on a frigid, windy night, they arrived as a ragtag group of eight snarly looking Confederate escapees. On the outskirts of the town, they bade farewell to their companions who were heading to Milwaukee and made camp inside an old abandoned shack. After a short rest, they packed up and went into town. O-B did all the talking since he knew how to hide his accent better than the boys. They soon found a man who knew exactly who they were looking for and eyed the three young men suspiciously. He pointed to a two-story building right around the comer from where they were.

They made their way up the street and spotted a sign on the building that said Steve's Place. They knew they had found the mark. They walked up to the door and entered cautiously. What they found when they got inside looked like something out of the Wild West. There were all sorts of burly characters scattered about the place, and everyone seemed to be staring at them with the kind of interest that a person does not want. The place was a tavern of some sort, only most people did not seem to be drinking. They made their way through the hailstorm of ominous stares over to the man behind the bar. He was an enormous man with a pitch-black beard that ran down to the top of his belly. He was wearing a dusty brown cowboy hat, which was somehow reassuring to the boys and O-B, though only slightly.

As they approached the bar, they could smell the stale whiskey and cigar smoke that often infiltrated a tavern. The bearded man did not move nor take his eyes off of them as O-B begged to speak. "We're looking for Steve," O-B said as his voice quivered ever so minutely.

They all sat there staring at each other for what seemed like an eternity. Joe held on to the Derringer in his pocket with a death grip, not even knowing he was doing so. Just as the boys were about to make a mad dash for the door, the bearded man let out a booming cackle that seemed to echo throughout the whole place and rang around in between Joe's ears for a fortnight.

"Follow me," he said in a voice that was deeper than the lowest point of Lake Michigan.

The boys followed the bearded man around the end of the bar and through a door that was just beyond. They went through a small hallway and up a small flight of stairs to what they understood to be a living space above the "bar" area. The bearded man knocked on the door and a tall, stern-looking man appeared in the doorway.

The bearded man said, "These boys is lookin' fer you."

JJ looked up at their uncle, and all at once, O B included, noticed that he was a spitting image of Jim—only quite a few inches taller and years of hard living etched on his face. Steve sat there looking at the boys for a minute, who were too stunned to say anything at that moment. Finally his gaze crept over to Jim, and then back to Joe, and then again back to Jim.

"Uncle Steve?" Joe muttered faintly.

Immediately, Steve's eyes lit up, and he said, "Ha! I knew it was you boys! Come on in."

Joe felt a heavy, distinct burden lift from his shoulders and fly away like a dead leaf in autumn.

Uncle Steve was a stern looking man; however, they realized right away that he had their mother's sense of humor. As soon as the boys sat down, he quipped off an Irish joke aimed at both JJ and O-B. He said, "How do you get an Irishman on your roof? Tell him drinks are on the house!" He let out a loud chuckle that bounced around in the great room for a bit. Instantly, they liked him. It wasn't hard to tell that he could get anything he wanted out of anyone. He had an imposing figure and was also very personable at the same time. He was the kind of company that a person longs for after they have been down-and-out for a while. Just sitting there talking to him gave Joe an enormous amount of confidence.

Uncle Steve's place had a unique charm to it. The boys knew he was not married, but there was a distinct feel of the place being superbly kept by a woman. There were ornate lamps hanging on the walls and highly polished furniture made from rich mahogany and cherry wood. The windows all had fancy dressings, which somehow could not be seen very well from the outside. There were five bedrooms, a great room, two bathrooms with running water, and an enormous kitchen with a pantry that may have contained more food than the storehouse at Camp Douglas. Uncle Steve, as they soon found out, had a housemaid living there with him who cooked and cleaned and basically handled any house duty that might need getting done. Her name was Rosa, and she was an immigrant from Italy who spoke almost perfect English and was very nice to look at.

They spent many hours catching up with Uncle Steve. He wanted to know every last detail of everything, right up to the name of the guard that Joe almost beheaded the night they escaped from the prison camp. They were brought food of the likes they had not ever seen and delicious beer to drink. Uncle Steve had a passion for bratwurst, which Rosa fried in a pan and served with peppers and onions. The smell was divine and lingered in the air for a long time after they were finished eating. For dessert, they had something called strudel which was a German breakfast pastry which they ate far too much of.

JJ and O-B were in sensory overload and could barely keep their eyes open as they talked long into the night with Uncle Steve. Just as they were about to fall out right where they were sitting, Uncle Steve exclaimed, "Well, that's it then, tomorrow we will go to Milwaukee and meet with a friend of mine. There is a little project I have in mind in a town not far from there where you boys will do just fine,

I think. 'You get some rest now. Rosa has prepared a bed for each of you, and after breakfast, we will head north."

Before they got to their rooms, Joe and Jim exchanged a look, and they both realized they were about to begin a new life—a life of their own. It took seconds for Joe to fall asleep, and though he was out for almost eight hours, when Rosa came in to wake him, he felt as if he had been sleeping for minutes.

The breakfast that Rosa made rivaled Mrs. McSweeney's; however, the eggs were just not the same. They never were. For a moment, Joe had that sense of homesickness that comes when something reminds a person of a certain fondness for things they once had. They quickly finished breakfast, and Uncle Steve made a stop at a friend's house before they made for the train station. The ride was quick; it lasted less than two hours, and soon they were standing on a platform in Milwaukee Wisconsin.

Milwaukee was a wild town, and they had never seen anything like this place on Lake Michigan. It was quite a bit smaller than Chicago, but it had more bars, restaurants, breweries, and brothels. Milwaukee was right in the midst of being the grain trade capital of the world. Wisconsin was the second-largest grain-producing state in the United States, and more grain was traded in Milwaukee than any other place on the planet. It was a bustling little metropolis and was a real eye-opener for O-B and the boys.

Uncle Steve gave them the rundown. "You boys are gonna be headed north with me, to a town called Dundee. The railroad from all around meets up in that little town, and there is a need for some hospitality. First, though, we are gonna have a good time here in Milwaukee. Don't you boys worry about paying for anything, ol' Uncle Steve will take care of ya." They were all excited about living it up a little bit there in Milwaukee.

Uncle Steve took them to a ton of different places. They saw some theater shows, ate at some very fancy restaurants, and spent time in some of the numerous taverns that littered the landscape of Milwaukee. They drank beer from the local breweries and were incredibly impressed with how good it was. O-B was fond of a particular German brew called Best. Life was lived like never before—wine, women, gambling, food—all were available to them in great abundance and did not cost them a thing. At one point, Joe realized that he had not seen Uncle Steve actually pay for anything, but Joe thought he must have, there was no way all of these things were free.

On the third day, they woke, red-eyed and groggy, and got in a carriage with Uncle Steve. He took them to a place called the Cologne House, which was about six miles south of the downtown area. This place had a new world charm about it, and they could tell Uncle Steve was meeting someone there just by the way his mood had changed. He was no longer jovial and full of mirth. His business sense had kicked in. They all sat down at a table, and Uncle Steve went right up to speak with the tavern keep. After a few sentences were exchanged, Uncle Steve made his way back over to the table and said, "I'm going upstairs for a bit, you boys settle in and have a drink if you like.. Due to the previous night's shenanigans, they did not oblige. Uncle Steve headed upstairs.

After about fifteen minutes, Uncle Steve returned and sat down with the boys at their table. He had a big smile on his face again, and they all knew things had gone well upstairs. "Well, boys," he said, "we're gonna be heading out tomorrow to Dundee to meet the man that is going to sell us your new home. His name is Moran, and I really don't know much about him except that he's a shit-bird and will screw his mother into the ground, so I'm gonna need you boys to be sharp and keep your eyes peeled."

This kind of talk was something new, and suddenly Uncle Steve seemed a little bit more like what they had heard of him. Uncle Steve went on. "I'll have a little help up there, and of course I'll have my steel." Uncle Steve lifted up his shirt and exposed his very own colt .45 which none of them had seen to this point. "If I go to the big city or to a business deal, I have this thing on me at all times. You just never know when trouble is gonna come callin'."

The boys and O-B were no strangers to trouble, but they all shifted a little in their seats and prepared themselves for a wild ride.

The rest of the evening was spent much like the others. "Plenty of time to sleep on the train," Uncle Steve told them. "Live for today, don't waste it sleeping." They heeded the call and were out until just before dawn. They managed a few hours' sleep before Uncle Steve showed up to get them on the train to Dundee. They all slept on the two-and-a-half-hour train ride. The four days they spent in Milwaukee seemed to be more like eight to Joe. He was happy that

Jim was looking like his old self again, and O-B seemed to be enjoying the ride. While they were in Milwaukee, Uncle Steve had taken Jim to see a doctor who gave him some medications to ease the pain and help him heal. Jim said he felt much better and had a spring in his step that Joe had not seen since Tennessee. Everything was happening quickly now, but it all seemed perfect to Joe, like it was meant to be.

Dundee was not a big place, but it was packed together like all those taverns in Milwaukee. There were rows of houses and other buildings a hundred yards long, and the streets were practically filled with people. The town seemed to be buzzing for some reason. Joe could not figure out why but just assumed there was some attraction with this place that he had not thought of. The dust from caravans and lines of carriages filled the air with a dense fog and the sound of the train station echoed in their ears. Uncle Steve got their things off of the train and led them down the dusty path to their destination.

Two blocks from the railroad station was Moran's. Uncle Steve stopped right before they walked in and said, "I will do all the talking here, do not talk about the war with anyone here, they are mostly still loyal to the North so just avoid it. Tell them you are from Kenosha if anyone asks."

The boys and O-B nodded in agreement. With that, the four of them stepped inside.

Moran's was a place that catered to a seedy bunch. There were rifles and shotguns littered all about the place like snowflakes in a blizzard. Uncle Steve looked around and then called the boys to him. He said, "Don't expect this place to be like Milwaukee, these men have been booted out of most of the nicer places around here and this is where they ended up."

They knew Uncle Steve could handle himself, but there were a lot of men around and all of them looked like they had little reason to care about any laws. Still, Uncle Steve was an imposing figure. He was in his early thirties but looked much older, and the scars of hard living showed on his face like a road map.

Steve took a look around and decided on a table by the front window. The three boys sat down at the table while Uncle Steve went up to the bar and ordered them some beers. The barkeep was eyeing him suspiciously as he took care of the order. Joe noticed he had not taken his eye off Steve the entire time. The barkeep set the beers down on the bar and, in an ornery tone, said, "Two of your boys should not be in here."

Uncle Steve set some money down on the bar, grabbed the beers, and walked away without saying a word.

As Steve was heading back to the table, he turned to one of the customers who seemed to recognize him and said, "You know if Moran is around?"

The man told him Moran should be in shortly. Steve said, "Is he always late for meetings?"

The barkeep perked up and said, "Hey, it's only five after one, he'll be here soon."

Steve heard what he said but ignored him. Joe noticed the bartender eyeing up Steve with a menacing look. They sat there sipping their beers for around ten minutes when finally Moran walked in. He was flanked by two bigger blokes who appeared to be his bodyguards.

As Moran walked up to the bar, they all overheard the barkeep make a wisecrack about Uncle Steve and the meeting. Steve looked at O-B and the boys and said, "I don't like the way this is going, hopefully Moran will work everything out." Moran and his two friends came over to the table. They all reeked of booze, and Joe could tell they were mostly drunk. They all pulled chairs from the other tables, some of which had people sitting on them previously. Steve nodded and then introduced the group to Moran, who did not seem to care what their names were.

Moran's first words were "so you're the big shot from Milwaukee."

Steve just looked at him coldly and nodded. "Okay, let's get down to business," Moran said. "I have two buildings for sale down the street for one hundred fifty dollars apiece."

Steve cocked his head and said, "I was told less than that." Moran shook his head and called the barkeep over to order drinks. Moran ordered his drinks, and Steve called out for four more beers for him, JJ, and O-B. The barkeep gave him a smirk and said, "Those kids are done drinking."

Uncle Steve excused himself, got up, and walked over to the bar. He ordered four beers from the barkeep again, nicely and politely. "The drugstore is around the corner," the barkeep quipped. Before his rapier wit could complete the thought, Uncle Steve grabbed the back of his head and rammed it into the top of the bar. The barkeep was knocked out cold and lay crumpled up on the dusty floor. At once, the two big blokes with Moran got up and started after Uncle Steve. Before they got two feet, two men with long coats stood up, produced a couple over-under 30-30s and plugged two rounds into the floor directly in front of the bodyguards. JJ and O B were startled by this turn of events and Joe felt himself reaching for the tiny Derringer, feeling almost silly for doing so with so many weapons lying around. The two bodyguards looked at the tall men with long coats who were now leveling their rifles at their boss, and then back at Moran, who motioned quickly for them to sit down.

Uncle Steve marched back to the table, grabbed his chair, turned it around so it was directly in front of Moran, and sat down so his face was in Moran's. He said, "Let's start this deal over, shall we?"

Moran, who was somewhat of a coward and did not want to get shot, simply nodded. Steve turned toward Joe and asked him, "How much money do we have to spend on this deal?"

Joe pulled out all the money he had and somehow, without cracking his voice, said, "One hundred and twenty-three dollars."

Steve turned to Moran and said, "I will give you one hundred and twenty three dollars for both buildings." Moran looked again at the two men in long coats with their rifles aimed at his head. He said quietly, "I agree."

"Good," Steve said, "we will sign this deal tonight at the Wisconsin Hotel at 7:00p.m."

Steve grabbed the boys, and they quickly headed out of Moran's, followed by the two men in long coats who backed their way out. JJ looked at each other with that patented McSweeney look and wondered if they had suddenly gotten in over their heads. Uncle Steve read their minds. "This is what business out here is all about, fellas. Don't you worry about anything. I'll make sure you boys are well taken care of."

Joe was not all that reassured. War had taught him how frail and delicate life is, and he was concerned for his own at this moment. He could sense the same from Jim. Only time would tell how they would fare in Dundee, Wisconsin.

They headed over to the Wisconsin Hotel. It turned out to be right across the street from the buildings they were going to buy, so they scoped out the property as they were walking. They were both two-story buildings built with strong cedar timbers, connected to each other by a short catwalk on the second story. The corner building had a lot of potential with windows facing both streets. It looked like it may have been a butcher shop or general store at one time. There was a fancy ornate door with some English carvings facing the main street and another entrance around the comer for deliveries. The windows had cedar shake overhangs and were stained a reddish color that matched the stain on the door. There was a balcony where the former occupant had anchors for the store sign, which would work out nicely when they had settled in and decided on a name for the place. The building on the comer was designated the main area where they would set up the inn, and the other would be a storage area with accommodation for the boys and the hired help.

After they were finished checking out their potential new place, Joe asked Uncle Steve if there was a doctor nearby. Jim wanted to make sure he could get some of the medication the doctor in Milwaukee had given him in case he ran out. Steve pointed the way and told them to meet in the hotel lobby at six thirty for some introductions and prepare for the deal. As they were walking, 0-B asked them, "Did you know what was going to happen over at Moran's?"

The McSweeney boys gave him "the look," and O-B knew they had no idea what that was all about. They were all glad to be out of that place in one piece. After meeting with the doctor, Jim, Joe, and O-B were feeling pretty burnt out from all the excitement over the last few days, so they headed back to the hotel to get some shut-eye. Uncle Steve had other plans, but they knew he would wake them when it was time.

Joe woke early and got the other boys awake for the big deal. They headed down to the hotel lobby, and the two long-coat=wearing companions of Uncle Steve were sitting at a table waiting for them. The boys headed over and sat down at the table. The two men did not say a word, but nodded at them when they approached. Joe felt it was a darn good thing to have these fellows on his side. They were both very tall, likely about six foot five or six at least. One was a bit stockier than the other, and they both were gruff-looking and stern. The stocky one was chewing on a thin, unlit cigar and spitting the tobacco out on the floor. Joe was both comfortable and nervous at the same time, and as he looked over at O-B and Jim, he could see they were feeling the same way.

After a minute or two of sitting there in silence, Uncle Steve showed up through the front door. He made the introductions for everyone. The skinnier one was Mike, and the stocky one was Bob. "These men are very capable of handling any type of situation that may come up," Steve said. This was something that JJ and O-B had already figured out. "We met in Milwaukee about fifteen years ago, and they have been working with me ever since," Steve added. "That's all you need to know about these boys, but they are going to be helping you out here and assist in shaping up the business." No one had any problems with that.

At 7:00p.m., Moran walked through the door of the Wisconsin Hotel, sober as a judge and alone.

Introductions were made again, like they had never been before. This time, Moran acknowledged the boys and shook their hands, albeit flaccidly. After a little discussion about the condition of the buildings, they agreed to the terms and began signing the papers. By 8:00p.m., the deal was done. Jim and Joe McSweeney were the new owners of 150 and 160 Jackson Street, Dundee, Wisconsin. They finalized everything, and Moran went on his way. Uncle Steve watched him walk out, and as soon as the door was shut, he exclaimed, "All right, boys, let's celebrate! Drinks are on Uncle Steve!"

Smiles were exchanged all around, even from Mike and Bob.

After a few hours of trading stories and whiskey, the boys and O-B learned a lot about their new companions, though they would have a hard time sorting things out through the haze of the booze, cigars, and beer. By midnight, their companions were all chatted out (and mostly drunk) so they headed up to their rooms for the night. The feeling that Joe had is one he never forgot; that feeling that a young man gets when he is about to begin his adult life. It coursed through his veins and surged through his brain, even as drunk as he was. They agreed to meet for breakfast at 11:00 a.m. Plenty of time to rest up, though the boys were not quite ready yet.

Joe, Jim, and O-B were still spinning from liquor, lack of sleep, and just too darn much excitement to comprehend, but they were happy. By God, they were happy. So happy they stayed an extra hour in the hotel bar trying to hash out what had just happened that day. The morning would soon be upon them, but they could have cared less. They were business owners, and they were men.

They awoke the next day and came into the hotel restaurant for breakfast. They did not have any details about what Uncle Steve expected of them, nor of the business. The boys thought they were going to be operating a small inn; however, Steve had other plans. "Well, boys," Steve said, "congratulations are in order. You are now the proud owners of a brand new casino, restaurant, tavern, and cathouse."

He let those words sink in for a minute or two, as clearly the boys were not expecting casino and cathouse. Joe said, "We don't know anything about running a cathouse or a casino, Uncle Steve, are you sure we can do it?"

Uncle Steve belted out a chuckle and said, "Don't worry, Joe. I'll take care of the girls and the gambling, I just need you boys to watch over the day-to-day stuff, and soon enough, you will know all you need to know."

The boys all were reassured, and even a little excited to begin their new business venture. "Bob and Mike here will be watching your backs, and I have a few more trusted people who will be in on the operation. They will assist you in all aspects of the business, but you also need to know that this is your business and the final say will be with you—not me or Bob or Mike. My cut is 10percent of the take for using my men and women." Steve paused for a second and thought to himself. "I will take care of everything with your parents as well," he added, "but make sure and get them a letter as soon as you can letting them know you are okay and are with me."

Joe nodded and started thinking about how he was going to explain everything. "Don't tell them about the business though, I don't want them worrying about you and getting you into any trouble." All three boys nodded their approval. "Oh, and one more thing," Steve said. "You boys forget you're from the South—most people up here are fiercely loyal to the North and would cut you up in a heartbeat if they knew you was Confederate prisoners."

The boys already knew this. Something was on Jim's mind, and he could no longer contain himself. "Uncle Steve, what should we call it?" he blurted out.

Steve looked at him with a righteous smirk and said," Well, isn't it obvious?" He paused for a minute to let them guess, and after the wait had gotten the best of them, he exclaimed "JJ's!"

The McSweeney boys looked at each other with that same look they had always exchanged. It was settled.

CHAPTER 5

DUNDEE

Everyone was assigned a task, whether it was looking for carpenters, organizing stock, or just plain cleaning up—the latter which was JJ and O-B's main duties. The building was in good condition, but it needed a lot of work to get it "livened up," as Uncle Steve called it. The plan was to open in ten days. While they were scrubbing the inside of the place and making idle chatter, Bob overheard them talking about where the money was going to come from for all the repairs and stock. "Let me assure you," Bob said, "your Uncle Steve has many friends in many places, it'll get done, don't you worry."

In the next few days, the place started to come alive. The place was laid out in such a fashion that the different areas of interest were separated by archways and French doors. Though the three main areas were distinctly separated, there was nothing standing in the way of co-mingling between the different business ventures. As you walked in, there was a greeting area which resembled somewhat of a foyer. There was a hatand-coat area off to the left side of the concierge desk, and if a person wished to stay at JJ's, there was another desk for check-ins. To the right was the main casino area. There was a somewhat large archway separated by a plastered wall from the main foyer. The gambling area received five refinished card tables with red colored felt stretched over their tops and finished with mahogany trim. There was a roulette wheel and also a craps pit in the center of the gambling area, with the card tables flanking them on all sides. There was not a finer gambling set-up anywhere, and even the Monte Carlo Casino might have had to tip its hat to JJ's.

Past the gambling area away from the front door was a smaller room with a tavern set-up for those just wishing to have a few drinks, or get away from the hustle and bustle of the casino. The bar area was finished several times with a fine shellac that was polished to a super high gloss. The furniture was all of a pristine quality that the boys had never seen before. They were aghast when the furniture craftsmen and carpenters had finished and allowed the boys to see their work for the first time.

To the left of the concierge desk, through another fancied archway, was where the girls plied their trade. In the main brothel area, there were plush velvet divans that varied in color from blue to purple to red. There was a small bar that served drinks with several stools for idle conversation between the girls and their clients. Past the bar was a stairway leading up to the hotel accommodations. Up in the second floor were fourteen rooms of varying sizes for hotel guests, which could also be rented for shorter periods as well. There were three rooms that were designated for brothel use only, so that they would not have any problems with room availability. All of the rooms had hung wooden doors and washbasins. The beds were all made of the finest materials, with down pillows covered in satin. "Looks more like a honeymoon cabin than a brothel," O-B commented after seeing the plush accommodations. JJ's was definitely a step above the rest.

Once everything was mostly completed (nothing is ever fully completed), the place was set for the grand opening which would take place on April 30, 1863. The North Woods were starting to burst green, and the smell of the majestic lodge pole pine cracking out the first buds of spring filled the air with a sense of renewal and hope. This was lumber country. There were trees everywhere one could look. The railroad had already been built through Dundee, heading west to carry the local product out to the needy home-building pioneers.

Lumberjacks and railroad men littered Dundee like swarms of bees after a giant can of sugar water. It was home to about two hundred of the like, and the number would swell on weekends to over twice that. The town would be a "giant melting pot," as Uncle Steve once told the boys, for the next few years as the railroad moved through.

East to West and even North to South. Most of the workers came from Milwaukee and a few were from outlying colonies spread out around the North Woods area.

These people all needed some sort of entertainment when not pounding spikes or clearing land, and JJ's was going to give them just that. Steve sent ten men and six women to staff the finest inn in the Midwest that was to be JJ's Bar and Gambling House. The staff was well trained in their respective duties, and the only initial problem was keeping the boys from ogling the girls at length, which Bob obliged to take care of.

Things were starting to come together for the boys, and they were pretty much overwhelmed at all that had taken place and the future they knew they were in for. They had come a long way from the swim hole in Sumner, Tennessee. Though they knew Southerners were not especially welcome in Dundee, the boys and O-B had decided, after a dinner and a couple beers of course, that they would make trips down to Camp Douglas and gather up as many prisoners as they could. They would help them on their way or possibly get them a job in Milwaukee or Dundee. The thoughts of that horrific place still lingered in their minds, and once in a while Jim would have nightmares that ended with him waking up in a cold sweat and rushing for his bottle of Dilaudid.

This would be their way of returning some of the kindness that was shown to them in the last few months. They knew it might be dangerous, but Joe figured that they would have enough bribe money to keep the guards quiet and obligatory. Joe was not sure that Uncle Steve would approve, but they were going to do it anyway.

JJ's became the talk of Dundee even before it opened. The townspeople were in fervors about the place, and all the attention only delighted the boys and O-B even more. People were coming up to them at any opportunity and asking them all sorts of questions about who was working there, what kinds of things they could do, and always if they could get a sneak peek. The boys did not oblige many questions, since Uncle Steve had advised them to lie low around town until the bar was opened. Two of the locals were hired by Uncle Steve to work at JJ's.

First was the doorman. Ox was a huge man who weighed around three hundred pounds and always carried a pitchfork. He looked like a giant compared to Joe, and he even made Bob look small by comparison. Uncle Steve probably felt that size does matter when you are working the door. The boys all agreed that Ox was someone that anyone in their right mind would not cross, and with him at the door they knew they had the edge on any trouble. The other local that was hired was a slow-witted but very friendly cleaning man named Joe. He was well-liked within the community and always had a smile on his face. People from Dundee were constantly badgering Joe about what was going on at JJ's. They wanted to know what it was like, when would it be open, and most importantly who was going to be working there. There were quite a few people on the payroll at JJ's that the townsfolk had no information on. It would not stay that way for long.

The grand opening came quickly, much faster than the boys had expected. With everything going on their minds were constantly directed into different paths, and when the day finally came to open, it was a bit of a shock for them. They did not have much to do, which was something that surprised them, considering they were owners of the business. All of the jobs were filled, so there were no real duties for them to do, but they were the last say in any questions any of the employees had, so they had to be available. The opening was a terrific success, with more people than they could count coming through the door that day. Men and women, old and young all came to see what JJ's was all about, and they were all impressed. The till was overflowing with money, and at the end of the day, they were called in to count it all up. They could hardly believe their eyes. In one day, they had made more money than they had ever seen before—or even heard about. The smiles were overflowing, and they were carrying on like schoolgirls whooping and hollering all night long. At around 4:00 or 5:00a.m., they finally called it a night. Joe looked over at Jim and said, "Did you ever think we were going to make money like this on our first day?"

Jim replied, "I didn't think we were going to make money like this in our first year!"

"God bless Uncle Steve," Joe said as he gave Joe one final look. They both trotted off to sleep—painless, careless, and as happy as two men could be.

The next day, they had other things to worry about. Uncle Steve had sent them a letter with instructions on what to do with the money now that the business had made some. They were to take care of all the "red tape," meaning the sherriff, the local politicians, and the other hotel men to name a few.

"This is how it's done in business," Steve wrote in the letter, "you take care of these people and you won't have any problems. Forget about them, though, and you will have problems, and lots of them. Don't forget about them."

Joe and Jim spent the entire day courting anyone that might give them issues with large amounts of money. Everyone seemed to be on their side all of a sudden. "It's amazing what a little money can do, hey?" Jim remarked to Joe.

"It's not justa little money," Joe replied.

The word was spreading about JJ's. People were hearing about this bona fide gambling house tucked up into the Kettle Moraine State Forest where you could get good drink, fine women, and gamble to your heart's content. The only problem was that some of the seedier elements started finding their way to JJ's. It attracted the high rollers, but then the thieves and vagrants were soon to follow. Where you find one, you will always find the other. People were heading to JJ's from south in Chicago and north in Minneapolis. The buzz was everywhere. The next few weeks were packed solid at JJ's. They had to hire more staff, and they made plans to put in a restaurant because people kept begging them for food. They wired Uncle Steve, and he made arrangements for some extra staff to come up from Milwaukee. They would make part of the second building into a dining area and run food into the casino as well. Things were still happening very quickly, and it took the boys some time to catch up on everything, but they were learning the business fast and were starting to change. A month ago, they were teenage Confederate prisoner escapees, and now they were businessmen in charge of a major operation. Joe thought to himself that things might be happening a little too fast.

Joe was a little concerned about his brother Jim. O-B cornered Joe one day while Jim was away. "Your brother is acting strange," he said.

Joe replied, "Yeah I noticed too, it must be that Dilaudid. One minute he's normal, the next he's talking like crazy."

"I guess it's working though because Joe hasn't complained of any pain lately," he added. They had no idea how much Jim was taking, but he was making weekly trips to the doctor to get more. Now that they were making money—and lots of it—there was no way to tell how much Jim was going through. Joe did not want to rock the boat.

Instead, Joe spoke with Jim about making a trip down to Camp Douglas to free some prisoners, and they agreed it was time. They boarded a train and headed for Chicago. It did not take long at all to reach their destination. Joe thought of the weeks it took for them to get from Camp Douglas to Kenosha and thought of the Donners and wondered how they were making out. He thought he might send a little money their way when he was able to. The guards at Camp Douglas were unrecognizable to them now. The commanding officer had been replaced, and a whole new company of guards had taken over, none less greedy than the last bunch. They paid the guards four hundred dollars, and seven men were set free. None of them were interested in coming back to Dundee, so they sent them off on a few safe routes they knew of to get them past the Illinois border, gave them some rations and water, and headed back to the train station. Joe wondered how many of them would make it.

He was not without hope, but still a little doubtful that money was going to make good.

The war was going badly for the South, and even worse for the prisoners of Camp Douglas. Most people could sense that it was just a matter of time. There was never any "good news" regarding the Southern rebellion, and the Union was starting to win battle after battle. Chancellorsville and Vicksburg were costly victories for the Union, but they were steadily pushing the Southern army back, time after time. People farther north lost much of their interest in the war, now that there was little threat to their property or health. They all felt victory was not far off and began to think of it in passing only or as a figment of idle conversation.

When the boys got back to Dundee, Uncle Steve was there waiting. Joe saw the look on his face and knew that he had found out about their trip to Camp Douglas. The boys walked over to him sheepishly and prepared for the worst. "I thought I told you boys to keep a low profile," Steve said. "You're gonna get in some trouble and fix us all real good," he added.

Joe said, "I know it seems like it's foolish, but that place is awful and we want to help out in whatever way we can. The run was quick, and we never spoke to or saw anyone other than the two guards we bribed to get the prisoners out."

Steve looked at his two young nephews for a minute and then replied, "Well, my hands are tied here. There isn't much I can do to stop you boys from going down there and doing what you feel like is your duty." He added, "Tomorrow you are both gonna meet me in Chicago, there's a friend of mine I want to introduce to you. He will be coming up here to JJ's once in a while, and I want you to get to know him. Here's your tickets." Steve handed them two train tickets for tomorrow to leave at 6:00 a.m. "I'm proud of you, boys, and I understand why you want to help out with this war business," Steve said. "Shoot, no one could stop me from doing anything ever, why should I think I can stop you from doing what you think is the right thing." Steve smiled, patted Joe and Jim on the shoulder, and then stepped on the train. Joe and Jim gave each other the look and headed toward JJ's for the night.

When they finally got off the train to Chicago the next day, it was already 3:00 p.m. The boys were tired and weary from train travel, the hours of which they had lost count of. O-B had been left to watch over JJ's, so they had all but forgotten about it for the time being. They lumbered over to the hotel that Steve had told them to meet at, the Green Tree. The hotel was more of a tavern. There were a bunch of people sitting around playing poker and a faro table. They spotted Uncle Steve sitting at a table in the far comer with a few other gents playing poker. They started walking over, but before they could reach the table, one of the men stood up and started screaming at the man sitting next to Steve. He was pointing his finger and screaming obscenities loud enough for everyone in the bar to take notice. The obscenities became louder and louder, and the man at the table did not move the entire time, he just sat there calmly with his eyes fixed on the screaming man. The irate man pounded on the table and threatened to fight his opponent, and finally the man sitting next to Steve calmly reached into his coat pocket and pulled out a small pistol, much like the one Joe had and laid it on the table.

The irate man stopped dead in his tracks, looked at the pistol; and the man who now had a smirk on his face quietly made his way past the boys out the door. All activities resumed as if nothing had ever happened.

The boys looked at each other quizzically and made their way over to the table. Uncle Steve stood up and greeted them and introduced his gun-toting friend. "Boys, I'd like you to meet my friend Bat, Bat Masterson." Uncle Steve was not short on surprises. The boys had heard all sorts of stories about this gambler slash lawman slash legend of the West, but they never expected in a million years to meet this man in person. They both shook his hand with incredulous looks on their faces.

"Nice to meet you, sir," Joe said, still with his jaw hovering somewhere near the floor.

"Nice to meet you as well," Bat said with another smirk. "Steve tells me you boys are his nephews and got a little operation runnin' up in the North Woods. I'd like to have a look at it."

"We would be happy to have you up there, Mr. Masterson," Jim said.

"Call me Bat, boys—it's always Bat." The lawman said.

Uncle Steve perked up and said, "Bat is a valuable man to have around when the chips are down—if you know what I mean."

The boys both nodded, and once again had a newfound respect for the Uncle Steve. No story their mother ever told them could have explained the kind of man he was. They doubted she even knew half of the story.

The next morning, after a long night of drinking and carrying on, they boarded a train to Dundee—Joe, Jim, Steve, and Bat. Along the way, they sat and listened as Bat and Steve told fantastic stories about gunfights, gambling, hangings, and all sorts of incredible things. It was clear that Bat was going up to Dundee for a reason.

He was now within the circle. Joe was glad to have all kinds of support around, and just as he was taking it all in, he noticed Bob and Mike were on the train with them. He spotted the two men and stared at them for a good minute until Bob tipped his hat at Joe. He figured out that whenever Steve was out and about, Bob and Mike were not far behind. Joe could never figure out why, but these two men were as loyal as anyone could ever be. He thought it might be money, but money only goes so far. There had to be something else.

The weather in the North Woods was pristine. The temperature was very pleasant, in the sixties, and the ground was starting to dry up. Green was everywhere. The sun helped everyone in Dundee. Lumber was moved more, and the railroad depended on dry weather to facilitate its construction. Good weather meant good business, especially for JJ's. O-B reported everything running smoothly while they were gone, and the boys headed to their racks for some rest, while Bat and Steve checked the place out.

Dundee had a sheriff named Chris and three deputies. Though the boys did not know it at the time, Steve and Chris were old friends from Kenosha. When Chris heard that Steve was in town with Bat Masterson, he made a trip over to JJ's to pay his respects. The boys had taken care of Chris and his deputies handsomely, and he wanted to let Steve know that his nephews were doing well up there. Chris and his deputies would turn a blind eye to any occasional fracture of the law. They would put people in jail if need be, but most incidents were worked out behind the back of the jail, rather than inside of it. There had been a few occasions where Chris would have to intervene when trouble arose, but it was mostly due to Moran's folks coming over to JJ's and causing a ruckus. Ox had beaten one man so badly that he ended up spending a night in jail, only because Chris thought it would be for the best that he was not seen that night.

The boys awoke after a short nap and met Bat and Steve over at the Wisconsin Hotel. Chris was there also, who greeted the boys and offered to buy them a beer. Uncle Steve had a lot of friends, as the boys were quickly finding out. He also had a lot of enemies, which was the reason for Bob and Mike, who were there at the hotel as well, keeping an eye on things as usual. At lunch, Bat mentioned a few of his friends were coming up to Dundee the next day to visit him. These friends just happened to be Jesse and Frank James, of the infamous James Gang. Bat assured the boys and Chris that there would be no trouble at all, and that was all they really needed to hear. Bat's word was as good as gold, and they had Uncle Steve's word on top of that. It seemed like every day Joe and Jim were rubbing elbows with famous people. They were making friends in high places, or depending on who you spoke to, low places. Either way, the word was out about JJ's and the McSweeney boys.

Around the middle of the evening, Jim excused himself from the company and headed back to his room. Joe had noticed him wincing here and there and was always aware when he took a shot of Dilaudid. He became a different person almost instantly, talkative and jovial. O-B told Joe that he had caught Jim hunched over at one of the card tables, squeezing his side in pain. Joe decided he was going to have to talk to Jim about his wound and knew that eventually he would have to talk to him about his Dilaudid use as well. While the drug might be keeping the pain away, he could sense that Jim was becoming way too dependent on it, and something other than drugs might have to be done about his wound. That night, Joe confronted Jim about the wound. Jim said it was nothing and that he was just having some "discomfort" with it, but it was under control and he shouldn't worry. Joe obliged him for the time being, but he grew even more worried and hoped that things would not get worse.

On May 1, six men rode into town: Jesse and Frank James along with four of their comrades. The first stop was to see Bat at the Wisconsin Hotel. On one hand, the arrival of the James Gang was a total blessing for JJ's. Their appearance attracted much attention, and business would be great for them while the James's brothers were there.

On the other hand, the type of people they attracted was not always welcome, and Ox would have his hands full trying to keep order in the place. Bat took the Jameses over to JJ's and introduced them to everyone. Frank and Jesse took a liking to Joe and Jim almost instantly, impressed by their respect, initiative, and the fact that neither one had reached twenty yet, but were running one of the finest gambling houses in the Midwest. The inner circle grew a little more. The James boys returned the show of respect from the McSweeney boys by spending vast amounts of money in JJ's. Twice they bought every person in the entire place a drink, even those that did not want one. No one wanted to refuse a request from one of the Jameses, so even those who were against alcohol took at least a sip of their drink and pretended that they loved every bit of it. Notoriety can go a long way, even in the North Woods.

The sherriff had been a little tepid at welcoming such notorious robbers into his town, mostly because he knew they would attract a lot of ne'er-do-wells. After the first day of having them in town, the jail was full of drunks and boxers. Incidents at JJ's were cut in half, however. This happened wherever the Jameses went. They brought trouble with them, but it never manifested within eyeshot of Frank or Jesse. They may have been infamous robbers, but they were not keen on causing a ruckus wherever they were hanging out, and preferred polite, casual atmosphere. JJ's was the perfect place for them. It was gaining a reputation as being a classy and well-managed place. The word was "losing money at JJ's is a little less painful."

The McSweeney boys would politely take your money and not throw you out into the street. As it was, high rollers also loved the idea of being able to play a hand or two with Frank and Jesse James or Bat Masterson. The JJ's buzz was at a fever pitch.

One evening, the Jameses' gang was whooping it up at Moran's when one of the regulars stuck his nose into a conversation, telling the James boys that the McSweeneys were Southern trash, and "they should go back and die." The James Gang did not take very kindly to those words, and soon, Moran's was bursting from the inside out with fisticuffs and all sorts of violent happenings. Guns were drawn and shot. Three people were wounded in the ruckus. The sherriff's jail was filled with a dozen men, most of them too drunk to stand up. In the end, no charges were filed, but several dollars were paid in fines, and Chris now had a lot of work to do, which he was not happy at all about. He kept a closer eye on JJ's than its owners cared for.

Frank and Jesse were at JJ's when the altercation broke out at Moran's. The tables were full at JJ's where Bat and Frank James were playing faro with a businessman from Minnesota and some other regulars. Turns out the businessman was losing hand after hand to Bat who was playing banker at faro and was beginning to fume from all of his money disappearing. Bat was running an honest faro, but with all of the scuttlebutt about faro being a crooked game, the businessman had his doubts. Bat ignored him as much as he could, until after losing a big hand, the businessman threw his cards at Bat and cursed him. Soon Ox was at the table, pitchfork in tow. When one of the businessman's friends lunged at Ox, he promptly stabbed his pitchfork into the ground, mangling the man's toes. The cries were heard far and wide as the man and his ornery friends limped away to the jail. It turned out that the man with the mangled toes was a small town sherriff in Minnesota who was accompanying the businessman on his leisure trip. Chris tried to smooth things over, but he was swamped with the men from Moran's brawl, and the Minnesota sherriff left the jail cursing and hollering, vowing revenge against the "Southern trash" from JJ's and the Town of Dundee for allowing "criminals like Bat Masterson and the James Gang to run this town." Chris just chalked it up as another wild weekend in Dundee. He decided he was going to have to hire some new help.

The next afternoon, the James Gang decided to ride off, sensing the trouble that normally followed them was beginning to raise some unneeded attention for Jim and Joe. Before they left, Jesse pulled Joe aside and had a few words with him.

"Listen, kid," he said, "things are going bad for the South, and there may be a lot of trouble coming this way soon. I want you to know you've got our support, and if you ever need anything, you just give a holler and we'll be there."

Joe looked up at Jesse and smiled, almost dumbfounded by this show of loyalty and appreciation.

"I know what you're thinkin'," said Jesse. "We just appreciate the hospitality and havin' a place to come and wet our whistles when were up here in the north. You boys showed us a real good time and took real good care of us, and that's more than we coulda asked for." He reached in his pocket and pulled out a wad of bills and handed it to Joe. "Just a little token of my appreciation," Jesse said.

Joe looked at the wad of cash he was holding in his hand, more money than he had ever seen. He then handed the cash back to Jesse and said, "Consider it a down payment on any troubles that I might need your help with."

Jesse was thoroughly impressed by the manners of this green teenage businessman and said, "I knew you would give it back." He smiled at Joe who was still reeling a little from this exchange, but managed to smile back at the Southern legend standing in front of him.

"All right then, it's a deal," said Jesse, who gave Joe a whomp on the back. It was so hard it made him cough. They all rode off, letting the McSweeneys know they would be back soon when they had replenished their bankrolls. It was a bittersweet parting, though not so much for Chris the sherriff.

In the next few weeks, JJ's quieted down a bit, but Joe had another problem on his hands. He noticed Jim was gambling more, drinking too much; and Joe could tell when Jim was taking too much of his "medicine." His moods varied wildly, and he was almost like two different people, depending on when you caught him. When Joe confronted him about the drinking and gambling, Joe replied, "The alcohol helps my insides, and playing poker is much easier than working," which disturbed Joe a little more.

Bat had spent some time with Jim, teaching him how to read people at the poker table, and Jim had developed a strategy for winning at poker, which was actually working for him. Still, there was a problem with the Dilaudid use, as Joe would often lose track of Jim for days and then find him curled up in a hotel room somewhere in Dundee, begging for Joe to find him a doctor who had some medicine. To top it off, Jim asked Joe to remain silent about these episodes, though O-B and everyone else knew Jim was getting to be dependent on the drug and was having some problems.

After Joe had brought Jim back to JJ's one day, he went over to the doctor that Jim normally saw and asked him about the drug and about Jim. The doctor said he had been giving Jim far too much of the drug, and that Jim was becoming immune to it and developing an alarming tolerance to the drug. He also informed Joe that Jim was going to need an operation soon to try and fix his worsening injury before it was "too late," as he put it, which did not give Joe much comfort. The doctor said that the mood swings were caused by the lack of the drug, and that he could not keep up with Jim's use of Dilaudid, which explained why Jim would become withdrawn and reclusive. He had no painkiller and would go through a short period of withdrawal when he did not have the drug. The doctor also went on to let Joe know he was worried about Jim being cut open, stating that his experiences at Camp Douglas had affected him more than anyone knew and that the images were burned into his mind, making surgery just that much more difficult and dangerous. The doctor explained that the drug use was enough for Jim to "get by," but Joe knew that this was not going to last for long. He knew he was going to have to get Jim some real help, and hopefully take care of this injury once and for all. He also knew it was not going to happen very easily, and he would have to be very careful with how he brought it up to Jim.

On a slow summer night at JJ's, Jim and Bat were both at a table playing poker. Chris and his deputies had stopped in for their usual free dinner accompanied by their bribe money for dessert. Jim was in a garrulous mood, openly talkative about some things he probably shouldn't have been. It made him a difficult player to figure out for anyone at the table except for Bat, who was a master poker player. He never gave a thought to beating Jim; he figured there were always easy marks, and Jim was someone he cared about, why break him? Still Jim's use of Dilaudid did not escape Bat in the least bit. Joe was watching, and he knew Bat was taking good care of Jim, even at his most annoying moments. Bat had developed a real fondness for Jim, and it made Joe sleep a little easier at night.

Chris and his deputies were sitting at a table not far from where Jim and Bat were making short work of the other players at their table. The conversations were all in earshot, as the place was not as busy as it normally was. Chris overheard a conversation coming from a table adjacent to theirs, and his ears perked up. He looked over and noticed the sherriff from Minnesota with a few of his friends talking about how Jim and his brother were Southern garbage and should be run out of town. The fact that Jim was so loud and boisterous seemed to bother the Minnesota sherriff more and more. Chris could tell this was not going to end well. He stood up and got the attention of Ox. They both started walking over to the table where the Minnesota boys were sitting, but this time the small town sherriff was ready. He saw Ox walking over and threw his chair back, at the same time producing a .32 caliber pistol. He looked at Ox and started hollering.

"This place is a crooked gambling house!" he yelled. "This Southern trash got no place up here in the north! We don't need their kind up here, bringing all their crooked trash friends with them!"

Ox looked over at Chris, who was being calm and collected like any good lawman would do, and Chris motioned for Ox to take it easy. At the same time, Bat noticed what was going on and got himself ready for any real trouble. The Minnesota group all got up from their seats and escorted the sherriff out of the bar, knowing they were outnumbered and in for it, but not without the sherriff cussing and hollering all the way out of JJ's. This kind of ruckus happened often at JJ's, but Joe sensed that this guy would be back, and so did Bat and O-B. They all looked at each other with the kind of apprehension that followed a real warning sign. They would all be on the lookout from this small town sheriff with the big city mouth.

The next few days Jim spent in a town called West Bend, which was about twelve miles south from Dundee. On the fourth day, Jim sent a message to the doctor stating that he needed more Dilaudid and to have it ready. The doctor got word to Joe, and they decided to confront Jim when he arrived. On the fifth day, when Jim was supposed to arrive, there was no sign of him. Joe convinced the doctor to take a trip with him to West Bend, and they found Jim in the usual way: curled up on a hotel bed with booze bottles littered all around him. He looked ten years older than eighteen, and way worse than Joe had ever seen him. The doctor administered straight morphine, and Jim fell fast asleep. He had not slept in a couple of days, and he also had a badly broken wrist.

The doctor set the break as best as he could and fastened it with some makeshift plaster of Paris. Joe and the doctor loaded him on a buckboard and took him back to Dundee. Jim slept for thirty-two hours, barely moving the entire time. Joe kept a vigil over his brother, checking to make sure he was breathing every few minutes or so. O-B took over for Joe when it was time for him to get some sleep. Between the two of them, there was no leaving Jim's side. Joe was thankful to have O-B around. He had become like a second brother to him and was the person he trusted the most in Dundee. Joe felt like he would be able to fix his brother, but he didn't know if he could do it without O-B. They planned a fishing trip when Jim got better, hoping the fresh air and the lack of any gambling or booze would be just the thing Jim needed.

Jim had other ideas. He spent his "recovery" time up in his hotel room at the Wisconsin, ordering a few meals here and there and a ton of booze. One day, Joe came up to his room and nearly broke his ankle on one of the many booze bottles littered about Jim's hotel room. Joe stood there flabbergasted, and all Jim said was "what are you looking at?" With a menacing scowl on his face. Joe felt his brother slipping away. He knew the injury was really taking its toll now, but Jim was still only eighteen, and Joe had hopes that he would somehow recover from his wound and make it out of this. Joe had his doubts though.

Joe decided to take a trip down to Kenosha to see Uncle Steve and ask his advice. He left O-B in charge of the establishment and boarded a train on a sunny June morning just before dawn. Steve was waiting at the train station for him, and he knew why Joe had come.

"I hear my other nephew is having a hard time of it," Steve said coldly as Joe slowly got off the train.

Joe replied, "Yeah, he is . . . and to make matters worse, he's drinking damn near a bottle of booze every day. He just doesn't seem to care much anymore, and his pain is getting worse."

"I know a doctor in Milwaukee that might be able to help," said Steve. "He is a specialist in stomach problems, and he's been requested by people all over the country."

Joe nodded in agreement, and they headed over to Steve's house to iron out the details and partake in some of Maria's finest cooking. That night, Joe felt a little more at ease than he had been, but the lingering sadness of his brother's condition weighed heavily on his mind. He needed Jim to pull through. All they had been through together over the last year should have made them stronger, but Joe felt like it had only made things worse for Jim. He felt responsible for everything and desperately needed Jim to get better.

In the morning, Steve boarded the train back to Dundee with Joe. They decided it would be best to have Steve there, in case Jim felt like Joe was making this decision on his own. When they arrived, O-B greeted them with even more bad news. "Jim locked himself up in the hotel room and won't come out."

Joe looked at Steve, and they knew it was time to put their plan into action. Steve busted down the door, not before giving the hotel clerk a sufficient stipend to repair it with. When they got into the room, they were all slightly disgusted. Jim was white as a ghost and curled up in a little ball. The place reeked of booze and unshowered Jim. There was blood on his shirt where Jim had apparently been poking and prodding at his wound, trying to make himself feel better. Joe noticed a few empty bottles of Dilaudid on the dresser.

"All right, young man, it's time to get you some help," said Steve in his matter-of-fact voice.

Jim just looked up at him and started sobbing. Joe felt like hugging his brother and telling him everything was going to be all right, but he resisted, knowing he had to be stern with Jim, or he would go back to running away from the pain. They got Jim an overcoat and carried him over to JJ's where they gave him some coffee and a few pieces of bacon to eat. Jim resisted, but he feared the wrath of Steve more than his pain at that point.

That evening, they all boarded a train for Milwaukee—Joe, Jim, and Steve. O-B was left in charge again, to which he gladly accepted. "It's a damn bit of peace and quiet here with y'all running around Wisconsin," he said with his ear-to-ear grin.

O-B was becoming the face of JJ's. All the customers loved him, and he always had a story to tell. He was the master of ceremonies, while Joe was happier being the man behind the mask running the show. O-B made a good friend out of Ox, who loved to sit and hear him tell stories about the war. Ox held O-B in high regard as his father was a captain in the North army and had seen as much combat as O-B, if not more. If anyone took an ill stance with O-B, which rarely happened if ever, Ox would be there in a heartbeat, pitchfork in hand, brandishing it like a normal person would a billy club.

Jim fell fast asleep in their train car after putting up a mild fit due to his growing withdrawals from the Dilaudid. As soon as he was asleep, Joe ordered himself a beer and got one for Steve as well. Joe said little to nothing on the trip, and Steve sensed his worry and left him to ponder the situation. The clickety-clack of the train was like a clock in Joe's mind, taking him back to all of the glorious days at the swim hole, when things were simpler and worries were just plain nonexistent. He wondered if his "new life" was all it was cracked up to be. If he was to lose his brother, it would all be for nothing.

They all nodded off and finally woke up when the train came to a stop in Milwaukee. Steve got their things together, and Joe carried Jim off to the carriage that would take them to their hotel. Jim was looking a slight bit better and started to get some color back in his cheeks. He was more than a bit ornery though, and it took a verbal lashing from Steve to keep him in check. Once they got to the hotel, Jim plopped down on the bed and did not move. The lack of nutrition had basically made him tired all the time, and sleeping was better than boozing. Joe managed a smile, and Steve was glad to see it.

"Don't worry about nothin'. We'll get him all fixed up," he said.

"I sure hope so," replied Joe. "I *sure* hope so."

The next morning came quickly, and Steve called for a carriage as soon as Jim was awake. They didn't bother with breakfast and got Jim over to the doctor as fast as they could. The doctor was waiting for them when they arrived and shook hands with Steve before promptly getting Jim into the examination room. Joe and Steve sat in the waiting room for over an hour before the doctor came out with the news.

"Well," the doctor said coldly, "his colon has been slightly severed by the bullet, and the infection is so bad now that the colon is no longer useful and needs to be removed."

Joe felt a sinking feeling taking him over. "He can have an operation to remove the infected parts, but he will have to wear a collection bag the rest of his life."

This was not good news for any of them. Steve even felt a little responsible for not getting Jim to a doctor sooner. The doctor added, "I gave him some morphine, and he will have to take that for the pain from now on, that Dilaudid is doing more damage to his insides than it is helping him ease the pain." Just as the doctor finished speaking, Jim came out of the exam room.

"I ain't havin' no operation," Jim said. "I'll get some of this morphine, and I'll be fine."

Joe said immediately, "You're havin that operation, and that's all there is to it."

Jim looked at him for a second with a little contempt in his eyes and then said, "It's my body. I'm the boss of it—not you." He turned away from them and sat down in the comer.

Joe looked at Uncle Steve as if to ask what he should do. Steve just motioned for him to take it easy and suggested they would figure out a way to convince Jim to have the operation, but Jim was obviously feeling very depressed about the news from the doctor. When they were finally ready to leave, the doctor brought out a supply of morphine, and Jim was shown how to administer it. It made him zombielike, but it was enough to make him feel better and not more than that.

The doctor warned Joe and Steve to keep a close watch on how much of it he was using. "He'll get hooked on it for sure, so keep an eye on how much he takes and restrict it if you need to."

They thanked the doctor and let him know they would soon be back—or at least hoped so.

They decided they were going to stay in Milwaukee for a short time to see if they could convince Jim to buck up and have the operation. Steve made the arrangements to stay at a nearby hotel called Palmer's Place.

The first night, Jim basically stayed in bed the whole time, with Joe steadfast by his side. Joe tried to get Jim into a decent frame of mind talking to him about old times at the swim hole, laughing and joking about some of their former gaffs and blunders. Joe did not bring up the operation at all, but it was hard for him not to think about it. He needed his brother to get better there was no doubt about it. They talked into the late hours, and Jim seemed to enjoy every minute of it. When they finally nodded off to sleep, it was near sunrise.

The next day, they spent walking around the Milwaukee downtown area, stopping at a lot of stores and markets. Joe got himself a new leather wallet, and Jim scored a pair of brand-new leather boots. Jim was on the morphine, and it seemed to make him less moody than the Dilaudid; however, he was a bit spaced out and lethargic. Still, Joe was happy his brother seemed to be in good spirits and making normal conversation. Steve was happy to see his nephews doing better than they had been; he did not want to have to explain to Mr. and Mrs. McSweeney how he had ruined their boys' lives. He genuinely liked both of them and saw quite a bit of himself in Joe. He thought back to his younger days in Tennessee and was aware that his life had followed an eerily similar path as the two young McSweeney boys.

That night, they decided to spend a little time in their hotel bar at Palmer's Place. They had a couple of faro tables, a big round poker table, and a nice, well-rounded liquor collection. Joe was a little apprehensive about letting Jim have a few drinks, but that ended when Jim ordered a beer instead of his usual whiskey. They sat down at a table, and Steve quickly excused himself. He had run into a business partner and needed to have some words with him. Joe was talking to Jim about new developments at JJ's place when he saw his brother's eyes light up and become fixated. He almost got a little worried until he turned around and saw the object of Jim's attention.

Marty had been a waitress at Palmer's Place for over two weeks. She had lost both of her parents at a young age. Her mother died giving birth to her little brother, and her father was killed in the war fighting for the North. She went to live with her grandmother who was kind and loving, but Marty was a girl who wanted to make a life of her own. When she turned seventeen, she moved to Milwaukee and worked at the telegraph company for a short time until she ran into Frank Palmer who gave her a job as a waitress in her hotel. She liked the job, but she wanted more out of life. She often dreamed about having a walk-in closet and a wardrobe full of expensive clothes, going out to fancy dinners and expensive parties. She was a dreamer who loved the finer things in life, but she also had a motherly streak that followed her around, coming from the loss of her own mother and the fond memories that she had. The mother in her allowed her to be a great waitress, and all the customers were extremely fond of her. She was somewhat plain-looking but had an electric smile that could light up an entire room. Right now, though, she was smiling at only one place, the young handsome looking boy who could not take his eyes off of her.

She walked over to their table and greeted them in her usual way. She got through "welcome to Palmer's Place, I'm—" when the young magic-eyed gentleman stood up and interrupted her with "the most beautiful thing I've ever seen."

Joe looked at his brother with amazement. He had never heard him say such romantic things, and he was a bit taken aback, as was the flush-cheeked waitress. She had met some Southerners in her days at Palmer's Place, and there was no mistaking this accent. She was just standing there looking at him for quite some time before she uttered, "Well, I'm done working in a few hours, I'd be glad to have a drink with you."

"I'd be honored," Jim said as he bowed low. Joe rolled his eyes.

"My name is Marty," she said as she extended her hand.

Jim grabbed it quickly, kissed it, and said, "My name is Jim, and this is my big brother, Joe. It's a great pleasure to meet you, Marty."

Her cheeks became even more flushed. Joe sat there, shaking his head, knowing he was not a part of this conversation at all. She soon left to take care of her duties. Jim did not take his eyes off of her the entire time. Joe gave up trying to talk to him and headed over to play faro.

When Steve arrived back at Palmer's Place, he noticed Joe sitting at the bar with a fairly big smirk on his face. He walked over and ordered a beer from the bartender. "Where the hell is your brother?" he said.

Joe looked up at him with the same smirk he had been wearing and pointed over to a table. Steve glanced over and saw Jim and Marty sitting at a table, laughing and holding hands like they were bride and groom.

"Well, I'll be a monkey's uncle," Steve said in his best Southern drawl. "What the hell happened here?" he added.

Joe just shrugged and smiled. Steve sat there bit, flabbergasted, when he had a thought. He slapped Joe on the shoulder and said, "This could be the break we needed."

He walked over to the table and introduced himself. "Listen, we are going to be heading back to Kenosha soon, I was wondering if you would like to come with us?" he asked the young lady.

Jim said, "We are?" in his typical McSweeney I'm-not-sure-what's-going-on-here way.

Steve gave him a little nudge and said, "Yes, we are, how about it, young lady?"

She thought for a second and said, "Well, I have a good job here and—"

Steve did not let her finish. He flipped out an amazing wad of cash and said, "How much is your salary then?"

She stared in awe at the money Steve was holding for a good long minute, looked over at Jim who was still dreamy-eyed, smiled, and said, "I'll get my things."

She decided not to tell Frank that she was not coming back. She had been living in a hotel room and did not have much to take with her, just a few small items and some clothes. Steve got her a trunk to keep her things in, and in the morning, they all got on a train for Kenosha.

Marty and Jim were instantly in love. She adored his accent and his aloof attitude and her motherly instincts were just the thing he needed. They spent the entire time on the train completely entranced with one another. When they got off in Kenosha, it was arm in arm. The next few days they spent really getting to know each other, and eventually Jim's condition came up in conversation.

He did not tell her all of the story, and she could tell. Eventually, she found a time to talk to Joe about it, and he explained the entire situation to her and the urgency of getting Jim the operation. She took the hint right away and began working on Jim. Steve's plan was working like a charm. Marty and Jim spent a few days alone at a hotel, and when they came back, Jim informed his brother that he would be having the operation. Joe breathed a huge sigh of relief and thanked his Uncle Steve profusely. Steve did not need any thanks; he was grateful his nephew had finally seen the light.

Arrangements were made with the doctor in Milwaukee, and within a few days, they were all set for Jim to have his operation. He was somewhat hesitant to the idea of wearing a collection bag the rest of his life, but he wanted to do anything to make Marty happy, and she was very adamant that he do whatever it took to make himself better.

Jim had the operation on a Wednesday afternoon in July. He had to stay in the hospital a week to recuperate, and Marty was with him the entire time. She cared for him like a mother, but the love between them was something that Jim had never known before, and it made his recovery time a lot less. Jim was still a bit thin and frail, but now he was eating regularly, though it was not much and hardly enough to keep him healthy, but he was showing strong signs of improvement. Dealing with the collection bag was a whole other story. He had a hole the size of a silver dollar in his stomach, and keeping the bag on was not an easy trick. There were adhesives that he had to use to keep it attached, and they were messy and uncomfortable. It took some real getting used to, but with Marty's help, it became tolerable. Ten days in the hospital, and Jim felt he was ready to get back to his old life.

They arrived back in Dundee to some fanfare at JJ's. O-B had received word they were coming back and decided to throw them a "welcome back" party. There was a roasted pig, and O-B had hired a group of fine musicians from out of town to come and play for the weekend. Marty was welcome with open arms, and she was well-liked by all at JJ's. Though she was much younger than the working girls, her motherly instincts took over, and she was soon taking care of them. They started calling her Momma, and she was always around to lend them a helping hand.

Jim had not been happier than Joe had seen him in a long time. He and Marty would spend entire nights talking, laughing, and crying. Joe was glad that his brother had someone there to remind him about life. Jim had seen things in his life that men twice his age would never know. He was barely drinking at all, and he had all but forgotten about gambling. They were inseparable and extremely happy—and so was Joe. He had some hope for Jim's future, and now it was time to take care of JJ's.

While he was gone, Chris the sheriff had been by several times to collect money from O-B, and much more than had previously been required. Some of the James Gang had shown up, and Chris had used this as a reason to up his take. Joe did not like the way this situation was playing out, but there was little he could do about it. He had a meeting with Chris, and the sheriff explained that his work nearly doubled when the James Gang shined around. He had to keep deputized civilians on standby just in case they showed up. Joe offered him and his deputies free meals indefinitely and gave him a nice increase in payola, and he seemed to be happy with that.

Meanwhile, business was booming in Dundee. The railroad to the west had been completed, and trains were pulling in and out like ants at a picnic. Dundee was fast becoming a stopover for people travelling through and was marked by everyone coming through as a great place to stop and have a good time. JJ's was at the top of that list and was literally packed on the weekends. Trains would drop off loads of people on Friday and cart them all away on Sunday. JJ's was holding up its reputation, thanks to O-B, as a straight place to gamble and a great place to have a good time.

Reputation was everything, as Moran soon found out. Only the seediest scoundrels would take refuge there. The war was rarely a topic at JJ's, but others in town found ways to bring up the fact that JJ's was catering to Southern sympathizers, mostly Moran's doing.

Still, business was booming, and the McSweeneys were making a lot of money. People of all types—from men with manicures to men with black fingernails—were regular customers. Trouble rarely showed its ugly face in JJ's, but once in a while things had to be taken care of.

One sticky July day, some of the James Gang was there having a good time and even running a couple of the faro tables. Things were going well until a particular known face happened to show up drunker than usual and louder than ever. Joe recognized him right away as the lawman from Minnesota. In an effort to not make too much work for Chris and his deputies, they decided to leave him alone and let him mouth his way out the door again. He leaned in on one of the faro tables that the James boys were working. The nods were given all around JJ's, and even Ox stayed his ground, pitchfork in hand. Unfortunately for that night, the lawdog kept losing at faro, making dumb plays and then accusing the dealers of cheating. Three times they switched dealers to make him shut up, but he kept on yammering loud as he could. Soon he started in about Southern sympathizers, and then he just kept going on and on about how JJ's was harboring fugitives and catering to Southerners.

Finally, Joe had enough and walked over to the table. He slammed his hand down on the bar right in front of the lawman and said, "That's enough! If you can't shut up, it's time for you to leave."

The man looked up at Joe and then at Ox who was standing right behind him. For once, he just grabbed what was left of his money and walked out. Joe watched him go into Moran's about 9:00 p.m.

The rest of the night was fairly uneventful except for an incident with a three-hundred-pound businessman who was being entertained by two of JJ's finest. Around 1:00p.m.,a huge crash was heard all throughout the place. When Joe ran upstairs, he found the businessman lying in the hallway after he had crashed through the bed and then the wall it was shoved up against. The girls were giggling for hours. Poor Joe the Swamper spent the entire rest of the night trying to clean up the mess.

The trips to Camp Douglas were still taking place. O-B and Joe were only going, as Jim was spending a lot of time with Marty. As the tide was turning in the war, so was it turning at Camp Douglas. The guards were getting greedier and more belligerent. They wanted three hundred dollars per prisoner now and were threatening to have them locked up every trip they made. Joe and O-B figured they had saved over forty prisoners from that wretched place over the course of the spring and summer.

When they got back, Bat pulled them aside and let them know that he and Uncle Steve were starting to not approve of their trips down there. Several people had been shooting their mouths off about the trips, and rumors were starting to spread. Joe decided they would have to stop going down there. He thought of all the young men who would never have a chance at life again being locked up in that awful place, and his heart bled a little. Still, he had more important problems to worry about.

Jim and Marty were doing well together. Jim was still in quite a bit of pain and discomfort, but he was starting to eat more, and his color came back a little. He was as happy as Joe had ever seen him with his new girl, and she was the talk of JJ's. They spent nights and days arm in arm, and Jim was not seen at the bar nor the poker tables. She cared for him constantly, helping him with his condition and bathing him. They were hopelessly in love, and everyone knew it. Joe felt the weight of his little brother lift off his shoulders and finally felt somewhat at ease. O-B was becoming a bit of a Dundee celebrity, as well as Ox. The pitchfork did most of the work though.

Near the end of July, a man came into JJ's who had a missing thumb, and the opposite thumbnail was black as night. He sat down at the same table Bat was on, and Bat struck up a conversation. Turns out the man had known Joe and Jim from the swim hole in Tennessee. Bat waved Joe over and immediately, he recognized him.

"Bill!" he said out loud when he got nearby.

Bill was one of the five boys that grew up together swimming and fishing in the glorious hole. They had known each other since they could talk, and as soon as Jim heard about it, he ran over to the table to meet his old buddy. They sat and had a long conversation about everything, including the war. Bill had been holed up in Camp Douglas and escaped on a whim one day as the guards were busy with a minor riot. He told Joe that the conditions were worsening, and they were losing upwards of seventy to one hundred prisoners a month. The guards were beating the young Southerners senseless as often as they could. Bill spoke of another young man that Joe had grown up with and stated that he was being held in the dungeon due to some problems he had speaking clearly. The young man was John Munger, and they wanted a thousand dollars for him. Joe felt he had to do something. This was a friend from home that he knew like his own brother, and money could free him. Money was not the problem; however, it was getting caught that would be the end of it all—especially with the war winding down and the South losing.

Nobody thought the war would last this long. The atrocities at the prisons were widespread and common, and those good people out there did what they could to make things better. They would make a final trip to Chicago and free John with the help of Bill. He became part of the inner circle at JJ's, helping Joe the Swamper with the odd jobs and even watching the door when Ox needed a break. He was a fairly large boy, much bigger than he had been growing up. He was a "late bloomer," as O-B called him. For a few weeks, they gathered after hours and planned their last trip to Chicago to free their childhood friend. They even convinced Bat to go with, needing his help to find a place for John to recover. Bat, Joe, O-B, Jim, and Bill would head out to Chicago on an unbearably hot August morning.

They arrived in Chicago near nightfall, tired and weary from all the bumps and the smell of coal burning. Bat arranged for them to have horses through a man he knew that met them at the train station. This man would also be holing up John for his recovery. They rode off into the near darkness, knowing exactly which path to take, having done it so many times.

They were quiet and precise, and they made sure they were not seen by anyone. They quickened their pace a little when they got into the countryside and found a little clearing in the woods adjacent to the prison where they made an impromptu camp. O-B and Jim stayed behind while Bat, Joe, and Bill snuck up to a spot near the gate. They could see the guards laughing and joking, so they figured it would be a good time to make their move. Joe and Bill made their way up to the gate while Bat took a position with his long gun just off to the rear and left. They got within feet of the guards when they called out to them.

The tall guard responded, "Who goes there?"

Joe and Bill put their hands in the air and walked casually up to them. "What the hell do you boys want?" the smaller guard said.

"We're here for an exchange," Bill said calmly.

The guards eyed them up and down and whispered to themselves. They unshouldered their rifles and pointed them at the boys.

"We don't do that anymore—unless you Southern trash brought a bank with you," said the tall guard. Joe pulled out a wallet, from which he produced $1000 and laid it on the ground. "That's a thousand dollars right there, we got three men in the woods with rifles aimed at your heads, so don't think about trying anything. You get the money when we see John Munger," Bill said.

The guards looked off into the direction of the woods and squinted to see if they could see anything. Bat seemed to sense this .and flashed a pocket mirror in their direction. "We'll be right back, don't go nowhere," the smaller guard said.

They sat there in the warm summer air for more than twenty minutes when they finally heard some muffled voices and feet shuffling. The guards returned, and they brought friends with them. Joe felt a little uneasy, and he looked over at Bill who had the same expression. When they rounded the corner to the gate, there were two new guards carrying John. One of them was a huge burly-looking monster who looked like he had just gotten done wrestling a tiger. He had a scar on his face that was three lines parallel along the length of his cheek, as if he had been clawed by someone . . . or something. They could see that John was weak and frail, probably not more than ninety pounds, and Joe felt like he probably would not have lasted too much longer in there.

The burly guard spoke, "You want this piece of Southern garbage?"

Bill nodded in the guard's general direction.

"Well, since you want him so bad, how's about we make an exchange for people?" the guard said. "One thousand five hundred and you." He pointed at Bill.

"Yeah, I remember you, you little, shit bird. We didn't get any money from you," said the burly guard as he took a step closer to Joe. Bat knew something was up, so he zoned in on the burly guard's head. The rest of the guards seemed to get some confidence behind this display by the burly guard, and they crept closer, brandishing their weapons.

"Why don't you just step away from that money and lie down on the ground," the guard said as he pointed his rifle at Bill's face. Joe turned around and looked in Bat's direction. Bat decided it was time for some help, so he leveled his Henry Repeater right at the burly guard's shoulder and let one rip.

The other guards all scattered when they heard the sound of Bat's rifle. The burly guard felt the sharp sting of a grazing gunshot wound on the top of his shoulder and fell backward nearly on top of John. Joe knew what would happen, and he tapped Bill on the shoulder as he rushed past him to grab John. The two boys had John arm in arm and were about ten feet away when they heard the first gunshot in their direction. The guards had taken defensive positions and were returning fire. They were using cap and ball rifles still, so there was some time for them to get away, and Bat was capping off rounds in their general direction to try to keep their heads pinned down. It took the boys about thirty seconds to reach the tree line, but to Joe it felt like an eternity. They had left the money on the ground, and Joe did not care in the least bit. He thought it was funny how things that would normally bother a human being tend to change quickly with the accumulation of wealth. Bat grouped up with them, and they hustled over to the camp. They found O-B halfway there, a little concerned and came out looking for them. They made it to the campsite, and Jim and quickly got on their horses and rode off. Joe looked over at John, and he was barely alive, riding on the back of O-B's horse. He was pale and looked like his skin was going to fly away in the summer breeze. He was not more than a skeleton and hair.

Just in time, Joe thought to himself.

They made it to Bat's friend's house a little after midnight. Soon, John was in a warm bed and resting. The gang all decided to hole up in Chicago for a few weeks to wait out John's recovery and have a little fun to celebrate their last trip (hopefully) to Camp Douglas. Bat took them to a nice hotel where he knew pretty much everyone, and they holed up for the time being. Jim was sorely missing Marty, and Joe tried to keep his spirits up by getting together with Bill and talking about the old times at the swim hole. They ate, drank, and laughed for days while Bat was making his usual rounds around the city, keeping his ties up. Things seemed to be going well after the big ruckus at Camp Douglas, but trouble was never that far away.

Back in Dundee, JJ's was doing quite well. Marty was taking care of the day-to-day accounting, and Ox was handling any issues that came up. The staff at JJ's was top-of-the-line, and while everyone was away, they all upped their responsibilities and took care of business. Things were going smoothly until one gray night, the sheriff from Minnesota returned. He had a gang of six with him, and he couldn't have shown up at a worse time. He and his boys had been drinking all day at Moran's and decided to "go get some rebel blood."

Ox was out back taking care of another altercation with Joe the Swamper when the Minnesota boys walked in. Right away, they started overturning tables and shouting obscenities. Marty was scared but walked up and asked them to leave quietly. The sheriff just stared her down and finally after a minute said, "Where's your rebel boy-friend, bitch?"

Marty stood there for a second and did not reply.

The sheriff grew impatient and then screamed, "Where is he?" He grabbed his revolver and knocked her on the side of her face. She fell down and lay sprawled out on the ground, unconscious. Ox had heard the ruckus and walked in to see the sheriff swatting Marty across the face. He leapt for his pitchfork, but before he could make it there, two of the sheriff's boys pulled out their revolvers and aimed at Ox. A wave of uneasiness filled the air, and the entire place was silent.

As soon as Chris the sheriff heard that the Minnesota gang was back in town, he gathered up as many deputies as he could find and headed over to JJ's. When they got there, things had already gone to worse as they had Ox outside and began beating him. The Minnesota lawman was inside JJ's, yelling and screaming about rebel sympathiz-ers and how they should all be put in prison.

Chris's boys got the drop on the guys who were beating Ox out-side and got them into custody. Chris made his way into the bar and leveled his rifle at the lawman's head. "I think that's about enough," Chris said as he spied Marty, still lying unconscious on the floor. The Minnesota lawdog swiveled around and saw that Chris and one of his deputies had him sighted.

"Well, well . . . another sympathizer." He did not get another word out, when Joe the Swamper ran up and whapped him on top of the head with a wooden stave, and he fell to the floor, knocked out cold.

His name was Bulger. He had been the sheriff of a small town in Minnesota but had been run out years ago for taking bribes and beating prisoners unmercifully. He was a wanderer who had a small group of men that pillaged and plundered wherever they could. They all hated anyone from the South and did whatever they could to cause problems for anyone they thought might be a Southern sympathizer. Their reputation had spread in their particular rural area of command, and Bulger never lost the bad taste in his mouth for what was going on at Dundee. The first time he was kicked out, he vowed revenge and damnation on the McSweeney boys. When he awoke in the jail, Chris gave him the ultimatum: "Either you leave and never come back, or my deputies will shoot you on sight."

Bulger, who was not in a position to argue, agreed. And he and his boys were set free. Chris did not like letting them go, knowing Jim would be furious about what had happened to his girlfriend. Marty was bruised and a little shaken up, but the girls took good care of her, and she was soon back on her feet, much to the delight of everyone around.

While in Chicago, Steve paid a visit to Bat and the boys. He expressed his concern for them making another trip to Camp Douglas, but Bat convinced him this was the last trip, and the boys all confirmed.

John was worth saving and every last dollar they had lost on him. He was one of the crew. The last bit of the McSweeney boys' long lost innocent days as those things were now in short supply. The whole group spent their remaining days in Chicago living it up. They spent time in all the finest spots, and having Bat and Steve with them guaranteed they would be well taken care of. When they had their fill of Chicago, they made their way back to the house to check up on John.

It took John more than a few days to regain his strength. His first few days were touch and go, and the man taking care of him had a doctor come and visit to make sure he was going to make it. The doctor fixed him up with an IV and gave him some medicine to help him recover. After the damage from the prison had worn away, he recovered rather quickly and was up and around feeling like himself again. His age allowed for a lively spirit, and now that he was free, it came back with vigor. When they arrived, it was all hugs and smiles.

John gave them all his eternal gratitude and enough warm embraces to last them all for quite a while. They reminisced about all the old times and discussed the last remaining member of their little group, Christopher. John said he had seen Christopher ship off, and he wasn't sure what had happened to him. They all silently hoped he had not gotten swallowed up by the war.

They decided to take John in at JJ's, doing odd jobs and the like with Bill and Joe the Swamper. They arrived in Dundee on an overcast day in September, and everyone was glad they were back. Chris the sheriff took Jim aside and told him what had happened to Marty. He was more furious with Marty for trying to get in the middle of a madman and his rage. He was incredibly happy that she was okay, and when things had settled down after their initial arrival, the two locked themselves in a room and did not come out for three days. Joe and O-B got back to business, and JJ's was soon running at full strength again.

Things were still going well for the place, and the weekends were getting hard to manage with the constant flow of customers. The McSweeney boys had made themselves a gold mine, and the flow of money was making them richer than they had ever imagined. Steve was even impressed with his cut. The rest of the fall and through the winter, things went so well the boys bought themselves a nice piece of property with a huge house just outside of town and moved in, with Marty and O-B tagging along. It was hard for Joe to imagine that just a year ago, they were three miserable rebel-boy prisoners mired in a dismal hellhole without hope. Now they were well respected businessmen with a ton of friends and a river of cash. People were going far out of their way to get to JJ's and meet the McSweeney boys. Life was good.

CHAPTER 6

THE NEW MULE

Jim was doing well, especially since he had Marty to take care of him. Though he was doing well, he was still having his share of problems. The bag was cumbersome and hard to take care of. His pain was still there, though it seemed to be kept at bay with the occasional shot of morphine. Marty made sure to keep an eye on the drug intake, and Jim did not seem to be taking too much at any one time. Marty was his painkiller. Jim thought he might have found his bride, and he told Joe he was going to soon ask her to marry him. Joe was happy to hear it and offered his approval. It was spring in Dundee, and Jim thought he might ask her sometime near summer.

They had not seen Bulger or any of his Minnesota gang since that fateful evening last summer. Turns out he was just waiting on his opportunity to get back at Dundee and especially JJ's. Chris the sheriff was always keeping an eye out for him, as he knew the disgruntled lawman would return, he just did not know it would be in such an awful way.

It was a brisk spring night in the North Woods, and JJ's was spilling out into the streets. Ox had his hands full keeping the usual arguments from getting out of control. Around 9:00 p.m., a group of Bulger's gang, around eight strong, busted out of Moran's in a drunken rage and made their way over to JJ's. They pushed their way into the main gambling area and started tearing up the place. Ox took on three of them, and Joe the Swamper got thumped on the back of the head in the first couple of minutes and was out cold. Bat was away on business, and Uncle Steve was back in Kenosha at the time. Joe was having a quiet night at the house, and Jim was in the store room taking inventory so they were not around, but O-B was caught up in the ruckus as well, but these Minnesota boys were on a mission. The mission was to keep the men at JJ's occupied while Bulger himself worked out his evil plan.

As soon as the ruckus started, Bulger quietly crept in and spotted his target. Marty was waiting tables, and when she was distracted, as well as everyone else in JJ's, by the ruckus that Bulger's men had started, he quickly grabbed her from behind, put his hand over her mouth, and pulled her out back. She was kicking and screaming, but his grip was too powerful, and he soon overwhelmed her. When he had gotten her into the woods a bit out behind JJ's, he struck her with the butt of his pistol and dazed her. She still tried to resist him, but the blood was trickling down into her eyes and mouth, and she felt weak. This was fine with Bulger as he wanted her to be conscious. He pulled her face close to his and said, "Your stinking rebel boyfriend won't be here to save you now." And then he spit his tobacco in her face. She pleaded with him to stop, but his mission was calculated, and there was no stopping him. He ripped her clothes off and raped her out in the woods behind JJ's tavern and gambling house. Not to be outdone by his previous misdeeds, he proceeded to smash her in the face and head with his pistol until she was out cold. Soon the woods were silent, and Marty lay there in her own blood and the filth of the wrong that had been done to her.

Ox finally got control of Bulger's men, and not having enough help and time to gather them up, he just threw them out onto the street. Their job was finished though, and they just disappeared into the night as Ox threw them out. Chris the sheriff had gotten wind of the disturbance by then and had rounded up his deputies to take care of this Bulger business once and for all. Unfortunately, they arrived too late to do anything, as Bulger and his men were already on their way out of town. Chris looked around for any trails and soon discovered Marty out behind the tavern. Jim had made his way back into the gambling area and was looking for her when Chris came in and stood before him. When Chris took his hat off, Jim knew instantly what had happened. He stopped Chris from saying anything and just said, "Where is she?"

"She's still out back, I sent one of my deputies to go wake up the doctor."

Everyone witnessed the conversation, and a wave of sorrow swept through JJ's like an arctic wind in the middle of summer. Jim made his way outside and saw his soon-to-be bride lying on a buckboard, being attended to by the doctor. He wept openly and cursed himself for not being there. He swore revenge on Bulger and all of his men and screamed loudly into the night air at any god who might have allowed this to happen.

Marty was a strong woman, but she had been beaten severely. The doctor worked on her for several days, trying to get her to respond. She was put on several drugs with the hopes that she would revive. She had not regained her consciousness and her breathing was terribly shallow. She finally succumbed to her injuries on April 24, 1964. Her funeral arrangements were made, and the entire town wept for her. The funeral itself was a grand affair, with her casket carried in a procession down the main street of Dundee, with those closest to her in tow.

Joe the Swamper was devastated as he and Marty had become good friends over her time there. She had treated Joe with dignity and was always very sweet to him, something he had never gotten from anyone before. The girls were all broken up as well. The brothel business was put on hold for the entire time Marty was hospitalized and then for a few days after as they tried to make some sense of the tragedy.

Jim had been through a lot in a relatively short period of time, but this was different. He tried to make himself feel better with morphine and booze, but his mind was a mess, and no drug in the world could have consoled his sorrow. The only thing that offered any solace was to find this miserable piece-of-shit Bulger and make him pay.

Bat and Chris had gotten together and decided to put together a posse, unbeknownst to Jim and Joe, and go find the violator wherever he may be. Chris got a few of his deputies together, leaving enough behind to take care of business, and Bat borrowed a few of the James Gang who were more than willing to help. Frank and Jesse were too far away to help, but they sent their regards and offered their services when they returned. Seven men rode out only two days after the funeral, looking for Bulger and his gang. They rode through town after town asking questions and interrogating anyone they could find. Bulger's gang was well-hated all throughout Wisconsin, so it was not hard to pick up their trail. Bat got word they were holed up in a town called Mauston, making their way back to Minnesota.

When the posse found them, they were shacked up in an abandoned farmhouse. Bat wasted no time and busted in on them while they were sleeping. None of them had a chance. Two of them tried to arm themselves and were shot dead; the rest were beaten severely, and Bulger was cuffed and taken back to Dundee. When they arrived, Bulger was thrown into the jail while Chris decided what to do with him. He went to go see Jim, who had heard the news and was waiting outside.

Chris spoke first, saying, "Well, we caught him, what do you think we should do with him?"

Jim said, "I've already decided." He pointed over to the back of the jailhouse. Chris looked over at the contraption that looked like a saw horse and said, "What the hell is that?"

"That's a mule," Jim said coldly. "And we're gonna make that sonofabitch ride it."

Chris shrugged and agreed.

Jim had spent the last few days putting together his salute to Camp Douglas. Bulger was placed on the mule shortly after, with two heavy stones tied to his legs. He sat on the mule for twelve hours. At times, he would scream out in agony and hatred, so Chris gagged him after he got sick of hearing the condemned man wail in the night. Jim spent no time near Bulger, knowing he might do something rash and deprive Bulger of his agony. The thoughts were too much though, and right around lunchtime, he could not take it anymore and walked up to Bulger who was barely conscious and pumped two slugs from a colt .45 into his chest—and Bulger was no more.

Chris took care of the body, and the mule was left in its spot as a reminder. Jim took to working at JJ's to keep his mind off the loss of Marty. He was putting in twelve- to fifteen-hour days, hanging out with Bat at the poker table and working side by side with

O-B. Though he was occupied all the time, he still had problems letting go of Marty. Bat tried to console him with some stories of the loved ones he had lost over the years, but Marty was only barely over twenty years old and did not deserve to die by anyone's wicked hand—and this was the thing that bothered Jim. Joe kept a close eye on his brother and made sure he was not slipping into any kind of depression. Jim complained about his medical issues once in a while, but seemed okay on the outside. On the inside, he was completely tom up. What he had been through was more than most men could stand.

As the spring faded and the summer wore on, things were changing around Dundee. More and more people were moving in, and the railroad was bringing in all sorts of transients and hangers-on. There were a lot of unrecognizable faces all over the place, and the homey crossroads town was becoming a bustling hive of all sorts of activity. JJ's was still reaping the benefits of it all, but Joe could sense that things were getting harder to manage. With Jim in his state and the pressure of keeping things orderly around the tavern, Jim decided they should take a trip somewhere to get away from it all for a few days. Bat recommended a friend's place out on the Wisconsin River, which was around sixty miles west of Dundee. He wired ahead and let his friend know the boys were coming.

Joe, Jim, Bill, John, and O-B were all set out for a little respite. Bat, Ox, and Joe the Swamper were left to take care of things at JJ's. They packed up some supplies and other sundries into a carriage and headed west. Joe thought this might be the thing they needed. They were still boys and had been through a war and so many other things, he felt they just needed to be boys one last time.

On the way, Joe asked Jim how he was feeling. Jim informed him that digesting food was becoming a problem. Food was running right through him.

"I just want the food to be inside so it can work the way it is supposed to," Jim said.

Joe did not know how to answer him.

Suddenly Jim blurted out, "Nothin' to it but to do it!"

Joe smiled. He hadn't heard that from his brother in a long, long time. Hope was renewed, and he felt pretty good about the trip right away. The long trek to the river turned out to be not so bad. They made it there in a day, albeit a long day.

They arrived at night to a note on the door of the man's house they were going to stay at. The note said they should make themselves at home and enjoy the stay. Bat's friend would be out of town fishing for the week. The place was theirs. It was too dark to see the lay of the land when they got there, but when they awoke the next day, they were awestricken. There were limestone formations everywhere, and the water seemed to travel in and out of them like a snake through the grass. The beauty of the place was almost too much for them, and O-B spent the entire morning just walking around and looking at the landscape. This was a great place for them, as it reminded them a lot of the swim hole back in Tennessee.

Joe and Jim spent some time talking that day. Breakfast was good, but Jim did not eat much at all. Joe asked him if everything was okay, and Jim said "I'm okay, but my belly is constantly making noises, and I'm always cleaning myself." He added, "It's just really hard to concentrate when your insides are running your life."

Joe told him, "Everything will be okay, just hang in there and make sure you eat something."

Jim nodded in agreement. Joe thought to himself, his little brother should not have to deal with this and vowed to keep him going.

Jim added, "I just want to sleep, everything seems normal when I sleep."

He went inside to take a shot of morphine and then took a nap. After walking around the riverbank for a while, Joe caught up with O-B and talked about his conversation with Jim.

"He followed me, he shouldn't have to deal with this. He doesn't deserve this."

O-B replied, "Hey, you didn't make him follow you, stop blaming yourself."

Joe said, "I know, but I can't help feeling like I put him in this position. I'll do whatever it takes to keep him going." Joe was feeling the guilt of Jim's misfortune harder than ever before.

The next day was full of fishing, swimming, and laughing. Jim seemed a little better than the previous day, and Joe noticed that he ate a little more than usual. It seemed to be a constant wave of emotions with Jim. As soon as he was sure Jim was falling off the deep end, he would say or do something as if nothing was bothering him, and then when things seemed to be going well, it was only a matter of time before he withdrew and became reclusive and depressed. Joe had already committed himself to seeing this thing through, and his little brother was all he thought about.

Around the middle of the day, Joe was sitting on the porch sipping some whiskey when suddenly he heard the distinctive sound of a group of horses and riders coming up the trail to the house they were on. They were making a slow trot, but that did not extinguish his worries. He readied himself for trouble and ran and got O-B who was already armed and on the lookout. Jim, Bill, and John were still at the lake fishing and were unaware. As the rumbling and hoof-pounding became closer, Joe gripped the Derringer pistol tightly and a little bead of sweat came trickling down his brow. The pounding of the hooves seemed to synchronize with the pounding of his heart. The nerves overtook him, and he realized at that moment that he was not cut out for a life of trouble.

He may have had his moments, and he could protect himself, but he did not like the feeling of being in danger, where as some people like Uncle Steve seemed to welcome it.

The first horseman came around the bend, and Joe thought he might faint, until he noticed the rider and who it was. The rider was none other than Frank James, followed by his brother Jesse, and then a half dozen of their gang in tow. Joe came busting around the corner, not realizing he was still gripping the Derringer pistol.

Frank, being the man he was, pulled up the reins on his horse and reached for his gun. In an instant, both parties realized what was going on and stopped what they were doing. Frank smiled ear-to-ear, and Joe pocketed his pistol. Joe and O-B welcomed them all, and soon Bill and John were introduced as well. The James boys had brought a carriage with a bunch of booze and food. It was clear they were on the road for a length of time. They unpacked and brought a gift for Joe and Jim.

One of the James Gang was also a wood carver and had made a miniature version of JJ's place. The McSweeney boys were flattered and invited the whole gang to stay with them. Jesse explained they could stay the night, but they were having a meeting the following night at a place a little farther west from where they were.

Joe and his "entourage" were invited to go with them, and they decided why not? Bill and John were still amazed at the sight of the James Gang and their relationship with Joe, Jim, and O-B, so they excitedly nodded when asked to go. That night, it was smiles all around, and Joe could tell that Bill and John were a little star struck. The Jameses were wild, and the two young former Tennessee farmers were like little schoolgirls with a crush. The Jameses did not seem to mind the attention and quickly took a liking to John and Bill, though their respect still lied with the McSweeney boys and O-B.

The next day, they rode off with the James Gang west to a small town called Black River Falls. This North Woods lumber town was on the railroad line and was host to a few places like JJ's and a huge chain of waterfalls which were beautiful to see. They holed up in a huge house positioned on a lake just outside of town. This place could have been painted in a picture, Joe thought as they rode up. The sun was high over the lake, and the clouds in the sky were making odd shapes against the bluest of blue skies. It seemed like something out of a dream, and Joe sat there for a long time and just stared at it. It was Jim who came out to him and asked, "Hey, man, what the heck are you doing out here?"

Joe was caught off guard and turned around quickly. He smiled at his brother and said, "Jim . . . just dreaming."

Jim seemed to catch on, and soon he was in the lake with John and Bill, laughing and whooping it up.

Jim felt good in the lake. It was exactly like it was before they had enlisted. The four boys were in the lake splashing around and playing their old games. O-B even got in on the fun. Joe and Jim gave each other "the look" several times that day, and they both felt like a little of their former life had returned for that time in the lake. Around dinnertime, they decided to call it quits and joined the Jameses and their gang for a meal in the house. Jim decided he wanted to stay out in the lake. Joe tried to convince him to get out and have some food, but it was clear Jim was having a "moment," and Joe decided not to push it and let him have his time out there. At dinner, the Jameses invited the JJ boys to the bar they were going to meet their contact at. O-B, Bill, and John decided to go, but Joe thought it best to stay behind with Jim.

Frank knew something was up with the McSweeney boys, so he pulled O-B aside. O-B explained what was going on with Jim and everything he had been through, and Frank nodded in understanding. "I suppose they won't want to know that JJ's was raided by some Northern troops just a day after y'all left."

O-B just sat there and shook his head with his eyes on the ground. "They made off with a day's earning and roughed up the place a little, but Bat was able to hold them off and wounded a few of them before he was run off," said Frank.

"I don't think we should tell Joe or Jim, they don't need to know right now."

"Nope," O-B said.

"We should just not tell them at all," Frank said. "Make sure everyone knows to keep it quiet."

O-B nodded in approval. Frank smacked him on the shoulder and said, "Now let me at some of that Tennessee whiskey you been hidin' in your hip flask."

O-B let out a hearty chuckle and reached into his pocket.

The rest of the night was spent around the fire, with everyone hootin' and a-hollerin' into the wee hours of the night. Frank and Jesse were telling the story of their latest train robbery and how they made the banker who was watching the money strip down into his under clothes and lay down in a puddle of mud. That was the thing that made it okay for Joe. He knew the Jameses were trouble and were likely being hunted at this very moment, but they had a style that was reminiscent of Robin Hood. They detested bankers and the rich snobs and appreciated the efforts of the common working man. Though he never saw the Jameses "give to the poor," they were more than generous with their money at JJ's.

Joe once saw Jesse James himself pick up one of the railroad workers who was unconsciously inebriated and lying in the middle of the street, carry him to a hotel, and cover his stay for the night. Earlier in the night, the man had complimented JJ's at the poker table that Jesse was playing.

Joe forgot what time they all called it quits and had a hard time remembering anything after they had passed around that huge jug of moonshine. His head was pounding from top to bottom, and he decided he needed to wash it off in the lake. He headed down with O-B to the lakeshore, and when he got closer, he noticed there was someone already there. When they got all the way to the shore, he realized it was Jim. Joe sat there for a minute, taken aback as he pieced together the conclusion that Jim had been in the lake through the entire night. Joe had not seen him at the fire and hadn't notice him come up from the lake to go to bed either. He may have missed him in the confusion, but it was not likely.

"Hey, little brother," Joe called out. Jim did not answer. Joe jumped in the lake and swam out to where his brother was standing, calm and peaceful as the lake itself.

"Hey, Jim" he said softly.

Jim did not answer.

"Have you been out here all night?"

Jim shook his head no but was silent still. They both sat there for some time without saying a word. Joe thought to himself that Jim was dying from the inside out. The breaking sun was peering through the trees, and from where Joe was standing, the faint light was creating a silhouette of Jim. He looked like a black angel standing motionless in the murky lake water. Joe had committed a long time ago to the well-being of his brother, and he was not going to give up now, not even if God and nature were working against him.

"This is exactly like it used to be," Jim said without moving a muscle. The voice seemed like it came out of the depths of the lake, as nebulous as the water it seemed to emanate from.

"That time is gone," Joe said quietly, "things are different now." Joe didn't mean to cast an ominous shadow, but he wanted Jim to snap back to reality. He was willing to try anything. "I just can't get over how fast things happened," Joe said. "It seems like yesterday we left on that train for Somers."

Joe thought to himself without saying anything, and then it hit him.

"Do you wanna go back home?" Joe said, hoping his brother might rally with the idea of Mrs. McSweeney's breakfast.

Jim said nothing for a minute or two, silently contemplating the idea that his brother had just laid before him. Finally, he decided, "Let's go visit them," he said matter-of-factly. Joe was happy to hear that sentence and immediately started making plans in his head for the trip.

Joe got his brother out of the water and even convinced him to have some food. Spirits were high for the first time in a long while. When the boys told O-B they were planning a trip to Tennessee, he jumped on the idea and soon it was a threesome making the trip to Selmer. They got Jim to rest up and planned to make the trip to Tennessee by train through Chicago and then they would rent a coach for the rest of the way to keep any suspicious eyes off of them when they crossed borders. The thought of seeing his mother and father again gave Joe a warm feeling inside that he had long since forgotten about. Often, when Joe would wake, he would think he was back in his old bed in Selmer, especially when he had first shipped off to war. He was especially delighted by the fact that he would be able to actually wake up in it for once.

Meanwhile, Bill and John were extremely taken by the James boys. They decided to follow them into the town for their meeting. Both young boys had still harbored a deep resentment for the North due to their treatment at Camp Douglas, and they fit right in with the James Gang who was, for all intents and purposes, fighting their own war against the North. The "meeting" at the bar turned out to be a knock-down, drag-out brawl when one of the bar patrons made a wisecrack at Jesse. Two people were shot, one was killed, and the bar was left in a shambles. Bill and John were no less taken by the James Gang, and for their courage, they were offered membership. Both boys agreed with open arms, and Jesse personally swore them in. They were official members of the James Gang now and would live by that code until the end of their days.

Joe was a bit sad to hear that Bill and John had embraced living as outlaws, but he understood seeing as both boys did not have any life of their own and the glamour of the Jameses' way of life was tough for anyone to resist. Joe told them they were planning a trip back to Tennessee, but Bill and John were going to ride with the James Gang back to Missouri and did not have much interest in going back home yet.

The next day, the James Gang—along with their two new compatriots—saddled up and headed off to their hometown, leaving Joe, Jim, and O-B to their own devices at the Black River Falls farm. The boys packed up their things, and instead of riding their horses back to Dundee, they decided to take the train. Jim was relieved to know he would not be bouncing behind a horse and loved the idea of a travelling outhouse and catered dining on the train. While they were on the train, Jim was at the bar having a few drinks when he met a Menomonee Indian named Grizzly. He was a huge man towering over Jim like a sequoia next to an elm. He had made a good living as a bodyguard for some rich bankers and had retired from the job. Jim thought they might be able to use another hand at JJ's, so he invited Grizzly to come by for a stay to see if he liked it there.

When they got off the train in Dundee, Bat was waiting for them. Joe and Jim had discussed making Bat a partner in the business, with him taking on so much responsibility while the boys were gone. It made perfect sense to both of the boys, and all they needed was Bat's approval.

"Well, damn, I thought you'd never ask," Bat responded with a smile when JJ gave him the news. "I have some bad news for you though," he said after the smile had worn off. "We have a new problem." Bat went on to explain that there was a murder of a patron of JJ's who had mouthed off about the South losing the war. He had left the bar around midnight and was found the next day strapped to the new mule with his throat cut.

"People have been talking, and JJ's has lost some business with this type of stuff going on there," Bat said. "Any more incidents like this, and I'm going to wish I never shook your hand," he said with a little chuckle.

Joe was concerned. He did not want JJ's to have the reputation of a place where people could get murdered. He went down the list of people who might have committed this crime, but could not pin it down to anyone. He wondered if someone outside of JJ's was trying to make the place look bad and thought of Moran and his antics. It just didn't make sense, though, for Moran to put himself at that kind of a risk. He might have been a mouthy miscreant, but he was also a businessman. It was troubling news, but hopefully Joe and O-B would be able to smooth things over.

Within a few days, everything was back to normal at JJ's. Joe had met with Chris, and they decided to keep a close eye on the staff at JJ's and also Moran's. For the few weeks Joe and the boys were back at Dundee, everything was going along fairly normal. The Indian that Jim had met on the train, Grizzly, showed up at JJ's, and they decided to take him on as a doorman to give Ox a hand. Grizzly and Ox became fast friends and ran like a well-oiled machine as far as keeping patrons in line. One was always looking out for the other, and Grizzly seemed to appreciate this new life that Jim had given him and was always thanking him for the job.

Joe and Jim decided they would wait a few months to make the trip to Tennessee, just to make sure things were operating normally and to give Bat a break from all the responsibility. The gold rush was in full swing, and anyone from the North that wanted a piece of the action was coming through Dundee on their way, and they never hesitated to make a pit stop at the famous JJ's. The place was back in full swing, and any ill-gotten reputation that might have been recently circulating about JJ's seemed to vanish as quickly as the summer breeze swept in.

Jim and Bat were spending a lot of time together. Since Jim still was embarrassed about his appliance, his interest in women was somewhat diminished, along with the fact that he had buried the love of his life. He replaced that love with gambling. Bat was never at the poker table long without Jim at his side. If anyone raised a concern about Bat's legitimacy, Jim was the first one to vouch for Bat. Jim was learning the "trade," so to speak, and was being molded by Bat whether he knew it or not. Jim was starting to learn all of the tricks and had become quite the poker player himself. Bat was not used to having someone at his side and felt Jim's loyalty was something he had never had but always wanted. For a time, Bat and Jim were virtually inseparable. Joe spent his days managing the business and keeping himself occupied with the day-to-day duties and making sure everyone was happy. The entire town was happy to have O-B back, and he was more than happy to resume his job at the front of the house. The girls were happy to have him back as well, having relied on their own laurels to drum up business. O-B was a natural and could have run any place in the world up the ladder.

July disappeared, and the sticky, humid doldrums of August was soon in full swing. Things were going along well, so Joe, Jim, and

O-B decided it was time to make the trip to Tennessee. They packed up all of their gear and headed down to the train station on a hot Wednesday morning. As they were leaving JJ's, Joe turned around to look at the place and suddenly felt out of sorts. He thought of how quickly things had happened from the time they had left the safety and comfort of the family farm to now. They had been away from home for almost two years, but the memories were still fresh in his mind. The pace that they had been going since meeting Uncle Steve took them a long way from the swim hole, but not that far. The taste of farm-fresh eggs was still on the tip of his tongue, even though he was over a thousand miles away from them. Joe was now considered a rich man, and he owed it all to Uncle Steve, and he could walk away from it all no worse for the wear.

Jim was a different story. Joe wished his little brother had ducked half a second sooner, but that was all water under the bridge now. Joe wondered how his mom would take the news. Just as he had that thought, Jim remarked, "Hey, let's not tell Mom and Dad about my stomach right away. I'm not ready to tell them yet."

Joe smiled to himself and gave his brother that famous look.

The three men boarded the train in Dundee headed for Chicago where they would pick up another train headed south through Illinois. Before they reached the border, they were to get off in Dix, Illinois, where they would meet up with one of Bat's friends who was going to take them by carriage through Kentucky and into Tennessee. The train was making its usual stops, and Joe had lost count of them, but he knew they were past Milwaukee and not quite to Chicago.

Joe was in the midst of daydreams about riding his old bicycle when he looked up and saw his Uncle Steve standing in front of him. "Well, looky here," Steve said with his patented smirk. "I think I found myself a couple of Southern miscreants."

Joe smiled wide as Jim, and O-B noticed Steve as well.

"Uncle Steve!" O-B exclaimed out loud.

Steve laughed a little and said, "Hey there Irish ."

Steve had decided to make the trip to Tennessee with the boys. It had been a dog's age since he had been there, and he was looking forward to seeing a piece of his own childhood. For a long time, he had thought about going back to see his sister and her family but was too busy with his daily "business" to consider it. After meeting the boys, it had struck him in a way he never could imagine, that he had missed out on something really important.

The train ride was full of stories, laughs, and of course, whiskey. Uncle Steve's "influence" had allowed them an entire train car to themselves, and they made the most of it. Jim was feeling a little better than normal, and he challenged Steve to a "serious" poker game. Steve was surprised how well Jim played and knew instantly that he was learning from Bat. They were going hand for hand for quite some time until Steve pulled away with an ace-high flush over Jim's royal straight. He might not have been the master player that Bat was, but Steve could hold his own, and Jim had become quite the prodigy himself. It was a match for the ages, and soon everyone got in on the action. By the time the train arrived in Dix, they were all three sheets to the wind and could barely walk from all the laughing and drinking.

They met up with Bat's friend just outside of the train station in Dix. The carriage was a bit rickety but large and comfortable for all four of them, and they were soon fast asleep. Steve had spoken in private with the driver before they started out, and Joe's last thought before he fell into a drunken slumber was wondering what he had said. He awoke groggy and stiff as the carriage was just crossing the border from Kentucky into Tennessee, though they could have been in Louisiana, and he would not have known. He saw that everyone else was still fast asleep, so he lay back down and tried to sleep off some of his hangover. He thought of the swim hole and how he loved that place so much when he was a child, and now it was just a fading memory. The countless times they jumped in and out of the water, the chicken fights, and the sunburns were still fresh in his head; yet he knew those times were long gone now. Still it made him feel comfortable to think about it. He hoped Jim would feel comfort in those memories too.

By the time they were nearing Sumner, Joe and Steve finally awoke from their slumber. Bat and Jim had been up for a time and were talking poker strategy. Steve nudged Joe and looked at him as if to say, "Check out these two" with a smirk as wide as the Grand Canyon. Joe nodded and chuckled a little. "I suppose you'll be stopping off at the horse track to make a wager or two," Steve said sarcastically to the happy couple.

Bat snorted and said, "Nope, just figurin' out how we're going to get the rest of your ill-gotten gains."

Steve looked at him a bit sideways and came back with "not in a coon's age, and certainly not 'fore I'm pushin' up daisies."

"Next week it is, then," Bat said as they all had a quick laugh.

The mood was light, and Joe could sense his brother was in good spirits. As they pulled up to the McSweeney farm, he could see his mother and father both standing there, awaiting their arrival. The trek up the path to the house seemed to take forever as so many thoughts were going through his mind. It was hard to know where to begin, and Jim made sure to remind him not to say anything about his injury. They all embraced, and Bat and O-B were introduced. Mr. McSweeney was honored to meet Bat, and also figured out that he knew O-B's father from his younger days. All of the McSweeneys immediately loved O-B, as did pretty much everyone else.

Steve and the elder McSweeneys seemed to get along just fine, and Joe wondered why he ever thought Uncle Steve might have been in disfavor. The way his father shook Steve's hand and the embrace he gave to Mrs. McSweeney erased any doubts that Steve was a welcome visitor to the farm. Steve's whole demeanor seemed to light up as he made the walk up to the house, and when the young Alice came bounding over the porch to say hello, Joe thought he saw a little mist in the eyes of his brave Uncle Steve. Annie was also there, she had come back for the summer to help out at the farm. Joe wondered for a bit which of the travelers this trip was going to aid the most. Jim hugged his mother for a good ten minutes, and right away she could tell that something was bothering him, though she neglected to say anything right away.

Right away, Jim and Joe set out for the swim hole. They left the elders to catch up on old times while the girls set up for lunch. As soon as they got there, both Jim and Joe felt a rush of blood to the head as they bounded off for the hole without a care in the world, as if time had stopped and God had sent them back a few years to relive these glorious moments they had long since forgotten about. They splashed each other and made catcalls. They took turns on the rope swing until they had blisters on their hands. Jim was careful not to disturb his bag, as he had tied a bandage around his waist prior to their visit to the hole, but he barely remembered it was there. Only a few sharp pains reminded him of his condition, but he thought little about it and even felt a little grateful that he was still able to swim about without too many problems, considering he might have had ita lot worse, or even have died that day on the hill overlooking Kentucky.

Soon enough, they were tired and hungry so they headed back to the farm. They walked up and met the rest of the clan getting lunch prepared. The look on their mother's face told them that she had something to say to them, and JJ gave each other a look; however, it was not the look that had bound them for so many years, this one was more like "uh-oh . . . . looks like the cat's out of the bag."

Steve humbly looked down at the ground, and JJ knew it was time to start explaining their whereabouts for the last two years. Over lunch, and then for a few hours after, they spent telling their parents everything they had left out of the letters. Mrs. McSweeney was a little taken aback at how exhaustive all the stories were, and how her two young sons had grown into professional men in what seemed like a matter of minutes. When it came time to explain how much money they had made, Mrs. McSweeney got lightheaded and had to lie down for a minute to keep herself from fainting. Joe handed his father two thousand dollars to aid in the household well-being and to help out with Annie's college tuition. He reluctantly accepted, but Steve explained a few times that the money was more than legit, and that there was much more to come, seeing as JJ's place was earning more than its fair share of Dundee money.

Between the three of them, they convinced the McSweeneys that this was simply a turn of good luck and hard work, and that they were well deserved of it. Though they were still a little bit skeptical, they trusted their two sons, who were being as genuine as they possibly could. Mrs. McSweeney sensed her brother Steve had more of a hand in things than they led on, but she was willing to accept that this was something her sons were proud of and that they had accomplished on their own, with possibly a little help from their uncle. Either way, it was going to be a grand visit. They decided to throw a huge party with a roast pig and all for the entire town of Sumner to enjoy. Two of the town's bravest heroes who made it in the North after being locked up in a war prison hellhole was a story that everyone wanted to hear.

That night, after dinner, Mrs. McSweeney cornered her youngest son as he made his way back from the outhouse. She knew by the color of his skin that something was not right, and after observing his eating habits, she felt it was time. He showed her his injury and explained how it happened. She wept a little, but at the same time felt extremely fortunate that she still had her baby boy alive and somewhat well. They talked outside for close to an hour, and Jim told her all about Marty and what had happened to her. Mrs. McSweeney felt sad for her sons; Jim for what he had been through, and Joe for the emotional toll that it must have taken on him to see his brother like that. They went back into the house arm in arm, and Jim was happier than he had been in a long, long time. Mrs. McSweeney was simply glad to have her boys home, even if it was for just a short time.

Something else was stirring in Joe. The whirlwind that was his life for the last two years had changed him, and he felt it. It was like a sledgehammer pounding on his heart, and it was relentless. Being home had only made things worse, and he knew what the outcome was going to be. If only there was a way to convince Jim and O-B to follow him. If things got worse in Dundee, it would help, but Jim and Bat were fast friends, and Joe knew it would be next to impossible to break that up. He felt his kinship with his brother slowly drifting away, but they were still blood, and that goes a long way, he thought. Either way it was going to be hard, and it was a new weight on Joe that only added to the worsening feeling in his gut.

The stay at home went well for everyone. The boys and Steve threw their party, and it was grand. People would be talking about that party for years to come. Mrs. McSweeney was a little irked at how "fancy" her boys had become and how they flashed their money at everyone and everything, but they were still just kids, and how else would they handle their success? The time had come to head back to Dundee. Uncle Steve promised to visit every now and then, and he kept that promise to the end of his days. The trip had changed him a little, "for the better," his sister would remark to him whenever she had the chance. The McSweeneys were happy to have their boys home but were both a little worried about Jim and his condition. Before they left, they stopped Joe, and before they could say anything, Joe looked them both in the eye and said, "Don't worry, we'll be coming home soon—for good." With that, he hugged them both, handed his father two thousand more dollars in cash, and hopped in the carriage.

While the troop was gone, things at Dundee went from bad to worse. The South was going to lose the war, and everyone knew it.

One Friday, a railroad worker who had heard that JJ's was run by Southerners was running his mouth about how he hated the South, and he got even louder when he lost his paycheck. "The South deserved to lose! They should all be in prisons!" he was heard screaming over the hustle and bustle of the gambling house. Ox walked over slowly and told him to be quiet. The man was having no part of it and belted Ox across the face. That was it for Ox, he brought his fist down on top of the railroad worker's head like a hammer, as he often did, and the man was instantly sleeping on the floor. Ox dragged him out back to let him think it through—unconsciously. The evening finished with no more problems, but when Bat was making his rounds, Sherriff Chris stopped him.

"Hey Bat, were you at JJ's last night?" he said.

Bat nodded and said, "What for?"

"We found a man strapped to the mule with his throat cut again," said Chris. "This is the second time now, this is becoming a habit."

Bat thought to himself for a second and said, "Well, Ox took him out back, but I was in there for the rest of the night, and Ox didn't move, plus I don't think he could kill a man like that." Bat thought to himself for a minute and then said, "Ox might be able to pound a man into the ground, but I would never make him out to be a killer."

Chris nodded in agreement and said, "Well, we need to keep an eye on this. Someone over there is taking things a little too personally."

Bat agreed and decided he would have to tell Joe and Jim about it, and maybe figure out a way to catch the mysterious murderer.

It did not take long for the news to spread throughout Dundee, and the day the vacationers arrived back in town, they were received with harsh stares and whispering amongst the townspeople they passed. Joe knew something was amiss as soon as he got off the train.

"What the hell is going on?" he said to Bat after giving him a big handshake.

Bat told Joe and Jim what had happened, and they all agreed something needed to be done.

Business was suffering, and many people who were regulars at JJ's place were now avoiding it like the plague. They resolved to keep an eye on anyone causing trouble and especially those Northern patriots who became violent and abusive, which was a good majority of their customers. It was going to be a real challenge.

Things were quiet for the next week. Joe and O-B did their best to reclaim the reputation that JJ's once had. They went around town and explained the situation to everyone they could, hoping there would be some return. Most people listened to what they had to say, but those who were keen to the knowledge that JJ's crew were all Southerners were not convinced. There was a real backlash by the townsfolk, most of which were Northern sympathizers. No one wanted to get their throats cut either, and with the incidents happening multiple times, there was a real fear that a person who was a little too loud might not make it to the next day.

After Joe and O-B spoke to Chris, the two were convinced that they needed to do act. What they were going to do was still up was the air.

The next day, things were slow at JJ's, but they were still making money. The brothel was always going to do well no matter what happened, and the town was still full of working stiffs relentlessly trying to turn their pay into a fortune. Around midnight, Joe was busy in the back going over inventory when he heard a ruckus coming from the casino. He came out to find four men cussing and screaming at Ox, pointing fingers and yelling Southern slurs at him. These four men were friends of the man who had been killed the previous week. Apparently, the word had gotten 'round that Ox was the last one to have contact with the man, and that was all the reason they needed to blame him for the man's death.

Soon, Joe the Swamper, the Indian, and Bat were surrounding the four men. They noticed the JJ's guard was on high alert, so they grabbed their things and headed for the door. Ox followed them and stood by the door, waiting for what he knew was going to happen.

Ox was no dummy, though he looked the part. A few minutes after they left, the ringleader came busting into the front door with a shotgun in his hand, but Ox was more than ready for him. Before the man had a chance to pick out a target, Ox clunked him on the head as he was well-known to do, and the man fell on the floor in a heap, shotgun sticking out from underneath his body. Ox picked up the man, slung him over his shoulder and carried him out back where he dumped him on the ground, much like he always did. For some reason, the first knock on the head did not do the job because as Ox laid him on the ground, he woke up, cussing and screaming much like he did before. One more bump on the skull, and he was out cold again. Just to be safe, Joe walked out at 2:00 a.m. and found that the man had woken up and was gone.

Around 10:00a.m. the next day, Joe and Jim were having break-fast and talking to some of the loyal JJ's regulars about the previous night's incidents when Chris the sherriff walked in. He came right over to the table where they were sitting and said, "Hey, Joe, anything happen here last night?"

Joe looked up at him and said, "Yeah, we were just discussing it."

Chris waved him over to the back of the bar. Joe told him what had happened with the four men and the potential gunman, the part that Ox had played, and the way they eventually got the situation under control. Chris looked at the ground and thought to himself a bit before saying "Well, I think you better come with me."

Joe agreed, but in the back of his mind, he felt he was not going to like the result of wherever Chris was taking him. They walked toward the jail and the around the back. When Joe saw the man straddling the mule, legs weighted down with bricks, and his throat cut, the reality of what had actually happened last night hit him like a granite block. Joe stood there and stared for a minute before he spoke. "This was the man that came in with the shotgun," he said quietly to Chris.

"I know it's not Ox doing this, he was in my sight the entire time, and when I went out at 2:00 a.m., he was still in the bar, and the man was gone."

Chris said, "Someone around here has a problem with people who hate Southerners."

Joe just nodded while his mind ran amok, trying to figure out what he could do to stop this. "Just stay quiet about this, I'll clean it up. We got the carnival train coming in a week or so, and I don't want any more trouble than I'm going to get already." Joe turned and headed back to his place.

Every three years, a large troop of animals and men made their way to Milwaukee from Baraboo, Wisconsin. The train passed through Dundee on its way, and there was always a huge gathering of people for the event. It brought people into town from all over the Midwest, and there was always a swarm of trouble whenever that many people were around. There were still rumors going around about JJ's, as well as a bunch of scuttlebutt about the war and the South's imminent defeat. People needed something to get their minds off the war, and the carnival train was just the thing. Chris, however, was going to have his hands full, and while he cleaned up the crime scene, he imagined his work was going to triple in the next few days, and he was right.

On Friday, the town was swelling with people ready to have a good time. Taverns and casinos were filling up like the whiskey bottles they were stocking up on. Chris had hired five extra men to help out with the trouble and act as deputies for the duration of the festival. By nightfall, people were everywhere in the streets, yelling and cussing and fighting and loving. JJ's was filled to the brim, and Joe had hired a few people himself to help with the influx of people. He had a few extra ladies as well, brought in from a brothel up north in a town called Hurley.

"It's going to be a wild weekend," he told his employees repeatedly. Some wondered if he was being optimistic or just cautious.

Things went surprisingly well at JJ's, but the same could not be said for the streets. The jail was nearly full, and they hadn't even made it to Saturday. Men and women were sleeping in the streets wherever they could find a soft piece of ground. Fights were breaking out left and right, but JJ's was surprisingly collected. Joe wondered if the rumors were causing the lull in violence, and suddenly felt good about his current situation—for a brief minute anyway.

Jim and Bat were busy all night at the poker tables, running up tabs and breaking wallets. Ox sat in a comer all night and barely moved. The place was raking in the dough, and everyone seemed to have a good time. They closed at 3:00 a.m. and would open at 10:00 a.m.to do it all over again.

Saturday was a repeat of Friday. The jail was completely full, and men were stacked on top of each other inside. Chris was setting his charges outside in the street with makeshift handcuffs and sections of rope retaining them. Drunks and drifters were setting up camp anywhere they could, and the new deputies had their hands full with complaints of stealing, loitering, and just plain drunkenness.

JJ's didn't fare quite as well as Saturday, however. Ox had to clunk several people on the head throughout the night, and a good-size brawl broke out on one of the faro tables. Out back, behind JJ's was full of knocked-out troublemakers. Bodies were littered all over the place, and Joe, as he made his rounds at the end of the night, personally made sure each one of them had a pulse. There were a few Southern haters amongst the mass of flesh, but JJ was too tired to keep watch over them and just crossed his fingers and hoped nothing would come of it.

Sunday began slow and peaceful. The town looked like a tornado had passed through with bodies and litter cluttering the open streets. People were everywhere, dusting themselves off and scurrying around to catch the outbound trains. The deputies were dragging the less-fortunate around by the scruff of their necks. The town smelled like one big hangover and looked none the better.

Chris was making his rounds and made sure he stopped by the back of JJ's. Men were propped up against the back of the building, lying in the bushes, and some even slumped over the horse trough. O-B and JJ met him out there to look over the situation. Chris called for his men to clean up the area, and the others looked around for any signs of foul play. Joe was walking through the woods and had some hope of coming out of this one clean when O-B called to him and Chris from a few yards away. There they found two men, the exact ones that Joe had remembered yelling Southern insults the night before, stretched out over a fallen log, both hog-tied, and both with their throats cut. The blood looked mildly fresh and was still dripping on the ground. The murders could not have taken place all that long ago. Joe shook his head and waited for Chris tosay something. "Let's get this town cleaned up, and then we can deal with this," Chris said. "We will have to find out what's going on here—one way or another."

Joe and O-B just nodded in silent agreement, and O-B went to get a knife and some blankets. "I don't want anyone knowing about this, and I'm sure you don't either," Chris said to Joe.

"No . . . . no, I don't," Joe replied.

Another man was found outside of Slim's with two bullet holes in his chest, so Chris had more tidying up to do, but by noon, everyone was out of Dundee; and the town was starting to resemble its former self. It still took three days to get everything back in order, but things were no worse for the wear. Chris buried three men without markers, and nobody ever knew about it. Chris asked if JJ's would stay closed for a bit until he had things wrapped up and formed a plan to catch the murderer. Joe obliged, without reluctance.

Joe was beginning to feel something he hadn't before. The trip to Sumner was where it had started, but it was real now, and it .was bothering him a lot. He was feeling a little in over his head, even though things were going well for the bar. Joe was not feeling the way he did when JJ's first opened—full of excitement and discovery, brimming with life and adventure. That feeling was long gone. The overwhelming situation with his brother, what happened with Marty, the James Gang, and now these murders to top it off were making him resent the whole thing. All he really wanted right now was a soft bed and a plate full of his mother's breakfast. The "'magic" of JJ's had completely worn off, and it took great effort to keep his thoughts optimistic about the place. He welcomed any respite from the place, and taking some time off because Chris said so was more reason than he needed to close down for a bit.

When he told Bat, O-B, and Jim about the shutdown, Bat informed him that he had won a chunk of land in Arizona over the weekend and wanted to check it out. "Let's take a trip!" Joe said without missing a beat.

The other tavern owners would be pleased as punch that JJ's was closed down, but Joe didn't care one bit. He was happy to get out of there and soak up some well-deserved rest and relaxation. He was excited to go, but when he asked Jim about it, he learned that Jim was not feeling well and did not want to make the trip. Joe did not like the idea of going to Tucson without him, but Bat decided to stay behind as well to hang out and watch over Jim. They both wanted to wait for the okay. from Chris to open again and get things going with JJ's.

Joe was still not fond of the idea as he had never been away from his brother for very long and was not sure it was the best idea with Jim's condition. Plus the bond they had formed seemed to be slowly slipping away. At first, Joe thought it was just "growing up," and they would be closer after it was all over, but there was something else going on. They had not given each other "the look" in a long time.

O-B, Ox, the Indian, and Joe packed up and got on a train for Tucson. They made the trip without any problems, and when they got to Tucson, they found a place called Big Jack's where they holed up for the time being. Big Jack's was similar to JJ's but about three times the size. The men cleaned up and spent the night there. The next day, they hung out at the tavern there and mingled with the locals. Arizona was a different kind of place, not something Joe was used to. There was a sense of lawlessness, but there was no war in the minds of the people, which was a welcome relief.

After a few hours, the word had spread that the owner of JJ's place in Dundee, Wisconsin, was there. Around dinnertime, they were presented with a round of drinks. The waitress let them know that Big Jack himself had bought the round for them. Soon, Jack made his way over to the table. He was a huge, stalwart man with a big burly moustache and a black leather vest that bared his name, Big Jack, embroidered over the chest pocket.

"How you boys doin'?" he said in a big booming voice, much larger than he was.

The conversation was mild at first with the two owners exchanging pleasantries, but soon the topic turned to JJ's place. Big Jack informed the group that he was Marty's uncle, and at first thought that Joe was the one who had married Marty and took her up to Dundee. They all could tell that Jack was not pleased at all about his niece's demise.

Joe and the rest of the gang were soon on their guard. Marty had never mentioned her father or uncle much, but it was known they did not like Southerners at all. That was most assured by her. Joe recalled her mentioning Big Jack's but did not remember until now. Joe looked over at O-B, and he seemed to be reading Joe's mind. It was almost time to leave.

Back in Dundee, Jim, Bat, and half a dozen JJ's employees were drinking and gambling at Slim's.

Though Slim's was a decent enough place, it had a reputation for trouble. Chris spent more time at Slim's than any other place in Dundee,—breaking up fights between Union soldiers and Southerners on a regular basis. Still the place attracted a lot of people, something Dundee was not short of. With JJ's being closed, the place was twice as packed. Jim and Bat were running the show on the poker table. Joe the Swamper was hanging out with some of the escorts. He often hung around them, and they all were grateful for Joe. He was like a big brother to many of the girls and was always respectful and courteous to them. Joe was dimwitted but exceptionally strong, and he acted as Ox's sidekick when anything went wrong, even busting a head or two when needed. Many people kept their distance from him for just that reason. The night was uneventful except for an altercation between a Southerner and a couple of Union boys. One of JJ's girls bought them both drinks and that seemed to calm things down. Slim's closed as usual, and Joe walked the girls back to JJ's.

That morning, Jim awoke to someone banging on his door. It was Chris the sherriff. "Come with me," he said rather stoically. They walked over around to the back of the jail and found two men strapped to the mule, both with the familiar fatal wound to the neck. Jim told Chris about the altercation at Slim's and identified the victims as the two Union boys that were in the altercation. He mentioned the differences were settled, but apparently the murderer did not think so. Chris asked him some questions about the Southerner they were arguing with, but that led nowhere as the man in question was an acquaintance of Chris and simply did not fit the profile of murderer, but he would eventually question him anyway. Chris's theory of a disgruntled Southern sympathizer was starting to make real sense. He decided to send Steve a letter, asking for some help. He had done so before, and with Steve's connections and his way of "getting things done," he would be a great asset in solving these murders.

STEVEN NELSON

In Tucson, things were looking no better. After Big Jack left the table, Joe overheard one of the waitresses say something about Big Jack and the "Southern trash" he was going to take care of. Joe was feeling uppity and decided to confront Big Jack. He walked right up to him and in his most authoritative voice said, "Look, my brother loved Marty, and she loved him too. What happened to her was tragic, and it practically ruined my brother for good. You can blame him for her death if you want, but when she died, a big part of him died as well."

The gang was startled by Joe's brazenness, especially considering Big Jack was nearly twice his size and surrounded by his men. Joe turned and walked away as Big Jack let out a big booming laugh. "Things have a way of working out, just like the war," Big Jack said as Joe walked past the table and out the door.

The gang followed quickly, and that was the end of their stay: in Tucson. Joe wired Jim that the gang was coming back and would be there in around three or four days. They never made it to Bat's land.

Chris decided he would tell Jim and Bat it was okay to open for business. Jim took the news with relish, wanting to get the business going again and get JJ's back to speed. Steve got the word from Chris and made his way up to Dundee that day. He let Chris know there was no outside word. "The murders must be happening from within," he surmised.

Chris agreed, and they set up their own plan to catch the killer. The bar opened the following day without much fanfare, and not too many customers either. The newest murders were talk of the town as the victims had been seen, and word spread quickly that it had something to do with JJ's and their Southern connections. JJ's was getting a bad reputation. Steve heard rumors all the way down in Kenosha, and though he left the business to his two young nephews to run, it was still connected to him and his name. Steve, Bat, and Jim stayed in the bar all day and made the most of the reopening.

Business was slow, so Jim was hitting the bottle pretty heavy. With nothing to do, it was easy for him to tie it on, and today seemed to be the perfect opportunity. No big brother around to curtail his extracurricular activities. Steve and Bat were busy discussing the murders and what they could do to trap the killer. Steve made his way over to Jim, who was busy at the bottom of a whiskey bottle, and

102

asked him about the murders. Jim looked up at him with laminated eyes and mumbled something in what sounded like Japanese and slumped down on the bar.

Steve chuckled a little and nodded to the bartender. "Let him sleep it off here, but keep an eye on him." Steve and Bat decided to take a walk around and have a look at things. They spent some time around back in the woods, checking things out. It was tough to see much with just an oil lamp, so they decided to wait until morning to investigate further. They made their way over to Slim's and had a beer out on the veranda.

They were in mid-conversation about Steve's idea on how to catch the murderer when they heard the faint sound of hooves pounding the dirt off in the distance.

Six riders came barreling into Dundee at around 10:00 p.m. They were all dressed in dark clothing, some had overcoats, and none of them looked like they meant well. The lead rider was an enormous man with a mutton-chop beard and a mean squint that made him look like he was always staring into the sun. He had a Union flag stitched into the shoulder of his overcoat and a silver colt .45 strapped to his waist. The riders slowed to a trot when they got within fifty yards of JJ's and then dismounted quickly right in front of the place. Neither Bat nor Steve suspected any foul play as they were deep in conversation about how to catch their elusive killer. Then something startled them. *Gunshots.*

Both of them armed themselves and raced over to JJ's. Bat was running like an Olympic champion, and when he saw the horses parked out in front of JJ's, he only assumed the worst. He got the drop on the lookout and, without warning, dropped him with a shot from his own colt .45. Just then, two men came busting out of the front door to JJ's and fired at Bat and Steve. The two sea-soned veterans jumped for cover as three other men soon followed behind. Shotguns and rifles were now being turned on them, but Bat had good cover around the side of an adjacent building. Steve had jumped behind a horse trough and kept low, occasionally firing over the top of the trough, hoping to get lucky. The dark riders were attempting to get on their horses and get away, so when Bat saw a lull in the firing, he popped around the comer and aimed his colt .45 carefully at the leader and squeezed. The massive man fell off of his horse and slumped to the ground. The rest of the men spurred their horses on and got off a few more shots just to keep Bat in cover. Bat was not about to be contained as he jumped out from his cover and ran over to the porch of the house where he took a rested shot at the man nearest to him and dropped him right off of his horse that continued to run off along with the others.

Chris had heard the shooting and got himself together as quickly as he could but arrived in time to see the dust that the fleeing riders had kicked up. He saw Bat bent over at the waist, trying to catch up with his adrenaline, and Steve was just getting himself up from behind the trough.

"What the hell happened?" Chris yelled at the two flustered men.

Steve looked over at the sherriff for a second and then walked over to him. "We don't know . . . go inside and find out what happened in there. I'm not going in," Steve said in as solemn of a voice as he ever had.

Just then, one of the girls came out screaming, "Someone get a doctor!"

Chris heard the cry for help and went running inside the once-pristine establishment. Neither Steve nor Bat spoke a word to each other for several minutes, but they were standing side by side. Finally, Steve broke the silence. "Your leg is bleeding," he said.

Bat looked down and said, "I hadn't noticed." In the flurry of fire, Bat caught a graze to his mid-thigh.

Jim had been on a bender all day. He was sitting on a stool at the bar with his head in his arms, barely awake. He heard the sounds of gambling in the background along with the noise of barroom conversation permeating the air. His thoughts drifted back to Sumner and the swim hole. He saw himself standing on the big rock, waiting to dive into the fresh clean water. The rush of the water hitting his face was all he could think of, though his thoughts were fuzzy at best. His injury was not bothering him at the moment, which caused him to think of his brother and that fateful day. He remembered his brother telling him to get down, but the excitement of what was happening froze him, and he was half a second too late. He wanted to tell Joe how this whole thing was not his fault and how he felt terrible about being such a burden. That was the thing that made him drink. It wasn't the injury, it wasn't the pain, it wasn't the life—it was the fact that Joe trusted him, and ultimately, he let his brother down. Joe was everything to him; he was the entire world, and all he wanted was to make his brother proud. What a failure he was. He thought of Marty. Sweet Marty, and what a horrible thing to have happen to her. There would never be any real justice. He wanted to bring her back. He wanted to see her again.

The men busted into the bar rather quickly and caught everyone off guard. Before Frank the bartender could react, there was a man pointing a gun into his eyes. "Where is the owner of this dump!" the man said to him. He was a burly man with a gruff beard and towered over nearly everyone. Frank froze and couldn't figure out what to say. He looked over at Jim lying on the bar, and that was the indication the burly man needed. Frank felt the sharp sting of a bullet entering his shoulder and fell backward on to the floor.

Jim barely heard the commotion around him. He was busy picturing the beautiful fall trees in the North Woods with Marty by his side. They were walking gently down the dirt road leading from the house to the little stream that wandered in and out of their property. They were talking of marriage and children. Things were better than ever. The brisk fall breeze was blowing back Marty's auburn hair, and the freckles on her face were glimmering in the sun. They were walking hand in hand, and her skin felt like buttercream on his fingers. She looked over and smiled at him. They stopped before a big lake, and it was water as far as the eye could see. He thought it was strange that they were standing in front of a lake. He looked over at her, and as he did, the fireworks started in the sky. He went to kiss her, and he could see the flashes of red, blue, and yellow in his eyes as his lips met hers. He wished he would never wake up.

It took hours for Chris to sort everything out. Jim's body was taken away quickly and placed in a casket outside of the sherriff's place. Frank the bartender and one of the railroad workers were treated for bullet wounds. There were no other casualties, other than those caused by the muzzle of Bat's revolver. It was a textbook assassination, and the target was Jim. Once the bar was cleared out and the streets were silent, Chris went to work. Of the two men killed by Bat, one of them was identified as the man who had shot Jim. Five rounds from his colt .45 had been aimed at Jim, and they all found their mark. It took one round from Bat's gun to kill the man, the bullet entering his temple right above his cheekbone. The mess was more than Chris could bear, but he kept on anyway.

The dead man bore no identification, but his horse did. Near the back of the saddle, embossed by a fine leather brand was the bold logo of Big Jack's Ranch. The surviving member of Bat's marksmanship was treated and brought into the sherriff's station for questioning. After several hours of "questioning" and a stint on the mule, the man confessed to being hired by Big Jack Wallich to gun down the owner of JJ's place. He had no idea that there was more than one owner of the bar, and apparently neither did Jack—until Joe showed up in Arizona. The big burly man turned out to be John Wallich, Big Jack's brother and Marty's father. Both men were reported to hate Southerners with a wild passion, and there were many murders of men from the South that were rumored to have been sponsored by the Wallich clan yet never solved. Chris locked up the prisoner, and he would stay in custody for a long, long time. Bat eventually got the names of the entire posse.

Joe was strangely silent the whole train ride back to Dundee. O-B thought Joe must have been shaken up by the incident at Big Jack's, but it was something else. Joe didn't know himself, until he stepped off the train onto the Dundee platform. As Uncle Steve explained what happened, Joe felt that he knew inside. He felt he knew the moment it happened, and he couldn't speak or feel anything at all. He was numb. Numb from all of the things that he had experienced over the last few years. He was surprised at his lack of emotion, but knew even at that moment, that he would never get over this. He wanted to trade every last dollar that he made for a chance to rewind time, a chance to walk away from everything. That was really what he wanted now, but at the same time, he knew that would never happen, and his anger started to surface. After Steve had finished and turned away, Joe looked at O-B with a light in his eyes that had never been seen and said, "That was what Jack meant when he said 'things have a way of working out'—this is not over."

He spent the next few hours talking with Steve, Bat, Chris, and O-B. Steve and Bat expressed their ideas for catching the murderer, and Joe was on board. They would stage a fight and hopefully catch their man red-handed. Steve hired a man from Kenosha to make the drive up and play the part of the victim. The fight would happen in JJ's place at night, and Ox would be in on it as well. Steve was a little worried about Joe and pulled him aside after the discussions were finished. Joe had not shown much emotion since hearing the news, and Steve was worried he was holding it in.

"You know it's all right if you need some time, Joe," Steve said. "Take a few weeks and get away for a little bit," he added.

Joe sat silent for a minute, looked up at Steve from where he was sitting, and replied, "I'm fine, Uncle Steve. We're gonna catch this killer, and then we're gonna pay a visit to Big Jack. That's that."

Steve nodded in agreement.

Joe decided they would have a funeral in Dundee, and then after all matters were settled, he would take the body back to Tennessee for proper burial. The townspeople came out in droves to pay their respects to Jim. Even the folks who had once condemned JJ's and their owners felt that Jim's demise was unwarranted and tragic. Joe was impressed with the outpouring of support and condolences. He felt the emptiness fade away for a little while. The James brothers came into town the next day and brought most of their gang, including the two boys from Sumner. Joe spoke little and ate even less. Most folks, including O-B, gave him plenty of space and did not bother him for any reason other than to offer their sympathies. Joe was grateful.

The funeral procession was magnificent to grandiose. A fancy oak carriage bore the body of Jim McSweeney drawn by six formally dressed Clydesdale horses. Everyone in town, including Moran, came out to watch the parade of mourning. Flowers were littered over the streets like leaves in the autumn wither. Joe was at the head of the procession. He did not look at or speak to anyone, though every few seconds someone from the crowd addressed him and his loss. He was followed by O-B, Steve, Bat, and Ox. After that, there was Joe the Swamper, the Indian, the girls, and employees of JJ's, and even Chris got his Sunday best on and joined the soft parade. The carriage made its way to a makeshift sarcophagus in the town cemetery, where a local priest paid Jim McSweeney his last respects. Sometime later, a stone would be placed in that very spot, though no body lay underneath it, heralding the death of one of Dundee's most favorite citizens. That stone would mark Jim's memory for over a hundred years and still remains to this day.

That night, Joe had retired to his home and made himself a small fire to sit by and think. He couldn't gather much of his thoughts; he just kept reliving the last few years over and over in his head, trying to figure out what went wrong. Suddenly he felt a hand on his shoulder; it was Uncle Steve.

"Look," he said. "I know you want to turn back the clock and change things, but life is just not like that Joe. You can blame yourself and everyone else in the world all you want, but it's not going to bring him back. I've lost quite a few friends over the years, and by all rights, I should be up there with them, but I'm not. I'm here, and so are you." Steve went on. "I suppose you're worried about what to tell your parents."

Joe realized he hadn't even thought about it.

"Tomorrow I'm going to get on a train to Sumner and tell your parents that Jim passed away from complications from his wounds. They don't need to know anything about this, and they knew he was not doing well anyhow, so it will make sense."

Joe nodded his head in solemn agreement.

"So it's settled then," Steve said. "I'll go to Sumner, and you'll go on living." Steve smiled at his nephew, who looked up and smiled back. Steve gave him a pat on the back and walked off, the chill Northwood's air following at his heels.

The plan to catch the killer would be put into action that next week. The railroad workers who were hired to play the fighters were briefed, and they rehearsed the act with Joe, Bat, Ox, and Chris. The two men would get in a fight over the typical North-South brouhaha, and then Ox would step in, removing the man from the North out to the back where he would pretend to bash him on the head. The man would then lie there as if unconscious and await the presence of the killer. They rehearsed everything down to the words that the two actors would speak and/or shout at each other. The plan was sorted out with every last detail considered; however, there was always the contingency that something may go wrong, and things would get horribly discombobulated, so they agreed on an abort procedure where the actor playing the victim would shout "Tennessee" as loud as he could, at which point Ox would get JJ's staff to clear everyone out, and the ringleaders would immediately come to the aid of the actor, whose name was Frank.

Joe was highly optimistic that they would catch the killer; however, neither Chris nor Bat were supremely confident that this would be a walk in the park. Also there was the unsettling notion that the killer would be someone close to JJ's, possibly one of the favored regulars or even one of the staff. Bat wondered if Joe would be able to come to terms with that result, but it was good to see Joe immersed in something other than the recent turn of events that had consumed his thought. The fact is, Joe was explicitly convinced that the murderer was someone he knew, but he told that to no one. Through the last few years of his life, Joe had learned that his instincts served him well, and he had begun to trust them. The trip back from Arizona had convinced him. He did not know for sure that his brother was gone, yet the emptiness that he felt inside led to only one conclusion. As he stepped off that train four days ago and saw Steve and Bat standing there, he knew his feelings were correct. Joe ran through the list of susceptible characters in his head but could decide on no one of them. He decided that no matter the identity of the killer, they were leading a dual life. It was not unheard of but made no sense nonetheless. He did not rule out any of the girls.

Saturday night came, and everyone was ready to go. The actors came into JJ's at staggered times to make it more believable. Joe, Bat, and O-B were positioned in a triangle to maximize their coverage. As the victim, Frank rose up at the poker table to confront the other actor—eyes were everywhere. There were several people present who Joe thought could have been the killer, but none of them seemed to care about the ruckus between the two actors. In fact, everyone there treated the situation as a regular, banal occurrence, as if it was normal. The two men shouting at each other halted the poker game and some of the surrounding activities, but most of the patrons barely blinked an eye. The two men went to wrestling, and then Ox stepped in. He grabbed Frank as Joe the Swamper grabbed the other actor. Since Joe the Swamper was not in on the plan, Joe McSweeney was a little worried that he might mistreat the other actor, but he did not notice the Swamper acting rashly, so he didn't do anything about it. Ox took Frank out back, and the Swamper took his partner out the front door. Frank took his position near a tree just outside of the woods by the back door.

The night went on normally and without event. Frank was starting to get uncomfortable lying there in the dark, damp woods as he waited in silence for something to happen. Joe, Bat, and O-B were mindful of everything that evening; however, there was not much to be mindful of. Joe paid Frank a visit outside shortly before closing time, asked him how he was doing, and bade him to be patient until after the guests had left and everything was quiet. Frank reluctantly agreed, and the scheme went on as planned. Closing time came, and the last of the patrons were escorted out by Ox and the Indian. The girls were closing up shop, and had bidden all of their guests farewell.

Joe was starting to get nervous. The killer had not shown himself, and time was running out on their big plan. If they did not catch the killer tonight, they would have to start all over again, and Joe was committed to seeing this thing through. The cleaning up had begun. The Swamper was sweeping the floor, and the bartenders were polishing the glassware and clearing the tables. Joe decided to take a walk.

He walked over to Slim's and passed Chris on the way, who was keeping watch over the streets. They talked about the lack of any activity, and both expressed a doubt about their plot to catch their man. "There's a lot of night left, son, let's keep up the watch."

Joe nodded and kept walking down the streets. The night was eerily silent, and the only noise was the crickets chirping and the leaves rustling in their hold, clinging to their branches for dear life as the Great North Woods wind attempted to sway their grasp. Joe thought of his brother, Jim, and the good times they had together. Joe had not quite realized how lonely he had become without Jim, even though they had grown apart some before his demise. It was not like they needed to be around each other all the time to know how the other was feeling. Joe thought back to grammar school and the book he read by Alexandre Dumas. It was a story of two conjoined twins who were separated at birth yet could still feel each other's emotions. He wondered if Jim was feeling his emotions right now, up there. He had been walking for some time and found himself a few blocks away from JJ's. He stopped for a second to take in the beauty of the night and how peaceful it was . . . and then he heard it. "Tennesseeeeee!"

Joe took off for the bar as fast as he could. As he passed Slim's, he could see a few employees gathered around, looking off into the distance behind JJ's. Joe got to the bar and stopped, his breathing heavy, and listened for any activity. He heard rustling and some shouts off in the distance behind JJ's in the woods, and he made directly for the sounds. He busted through the bush and stumbled a few times running through the woods. The shouts were getting louder, and he heard some wrestling on the ground. The moonlight was enough to outline some silhouettes off in the distance, and he could faintly see Ox's enormous figure standing still. As he got to the scene, Ox turned to look at him. He caught the glance and noticed that there was some deepening sorrow in the look. Joe looked down at the ground before him and saw Bat and Chris wrestling with a man. Joe sighed and decided that the killer had finally been caught. Bat had his knee in the back of the man, and Chris got up to look at Joe. When he was done, Bat got up and kicked the man in the side. As he did so, the man rolled over and presented his face to Joe. The sight of the man's face made Joe turn away in disgust. He looked at Ox and felt the pain in his eyes—it was Joe the Swamper.

Upon questioning, Joe the Swamper revealed he had been the only one involved in the killings. His anger for the Northern supporters had overtaken what little rational thought he had. The Swamper figured he was "helping to keep his job by getting rid of the troublemakers." Joe found out that the Swamper had been imprisoned at Camp Douglas for a time and possibly never fully recovered emotionally from his time there.

Chris would take care of everything, and the Swamper would be transported to a hospital prison in Madison where Chris had several friends. He would be forgotten about. Joe knew it was someone close but never thought it would be that close. Joe shook his head and looked at O-B who gave him a look that was strangely similar to the patented JJ look. Joe and O-B thanked Chris and headed off to JJ's for a nightcap. Bat was there waiting for them.

CHAPTER 7

DECISIONS

The next morning, Joe awoke with a certainty and confidence in his life that had been missing for some time. He met Bat and O-B at Slim's for breakfast. There he signed Bat into full ownership of JJ's, along with O-B who would return to Tennessee with Jim for a time. It was agreed that Bat would send money from time to time, against the will of Joe. He felt he had earned enough money in this business, but Bat would not let him rescind his share of the profits. "You were just as much responsible for JJ's success as anyone," Bat told him.

He also told O-B how much he would be missed while he was gone, and O-B promised to return in short time and continue his job as concierge. Joe was glad that O-B had found his lot in life, and it suited him well. They all smiled at one another and toasted their success and good fortunes, as fortuitous as they might not have been.

"There is one last thing," Joe said. Bat and O-B looked at him quizzically as if he had interrupted their joy.

"What's that?" Bat replied.

"Big Jack Wallich."

Joe sent for the James brothers. They arrived the following week, already bestowed with the knowledge of Jim's death and the capture of Joe the Swamper.

"Word travels fast," Joe said.

"It certainly does," replied Jesse with a smile. "Whatever you need us to do, we're here to help," he added.

JJ's had been slow for business once word got around that one of their employees was the murderer. Joe and Bat decided to close the place while they took care of the "Big Jack problem," as they called it.

The next day, they all boarded the train for the West to confront Big Jack and get justice, however it may come. The James Gang traveled by horse and would catch up with them in Tucson, or as it turned out, Joe's posse would catch up with the James Gang in Tucson.

Just forty miles outside of Dundee, the train they were traveling on broke down, and they were forced to travel by carriage to St. Louis, where they would catch the next train.

Joe was more than a little nervous. He was having second thoughts about this, and considering the nature of Big Jack and the other members of his crew, he wondered if they would ever accept captivity and the prospect of future imprisonment. He also wondered if the James Gang, specifically Jesse, ever would allow them to be taken alive. Jesse did not have any qualms about exacting his own brand of "justice" on Northern tyrants.

Further bloodshed was not a prospect Joe was comfortable with, but he felt it was out of his hands now. Bat and Jim were close, and this was more Bat's arena than his. Joe's anger was still palpable, and he decided whatever Big Jack and his crew got was what they deserved.

They rolled into Tucson a few days later. Jesse and Frank met them on the platform and got them out to their camp swiftly and without notice. The camp was an old abandoned farmhouse on the outskirts of town. The James Gang had been set up there for a few days and had already assembled quite a bit of intelligence on Big Jack's operation. He had twenty-five men working for him. On the fourth Saturday of the month, Big Jack would set up in Tucson for payday. The town was only five miles from Big Jack's ranch, and his men would spend the entire weekend in town spending much of what they had earned. This way, Big Jack had a great reputation with most of the businesses and town leaders and was fully supported by all law enforcement. It would be tough to take Big Jack down at most times of the month, but with payday approaching this particular Saturday, he would be mostly isolated from his gang. He looked to have no more than five or six men at the ranch during the weekend festivities. Joe was impressed with the information that the James Gang had obtained, but then he realized that Jesse and Frank did this sort of a thing for a living. It also occurred to him that this information would suit the James brothers well. They had only one reason to go to Big Jack's ranch on the fourth Saturday of the month, and that was to kill Big Jack.

The layout of Big Jack's ranch was confirmed by Ox and Joe, and then a plan was formed by Jesse, Frank, and Bat. They would surround and capture the remaining men holed up inside the bunkhouse. Joe, Jesse, Bat, and the Indian would then go inside the ranch where Big Jack would likely be sleeping. Big Jack had a big dog, and the Indian would take care of that first. Jesse would bind Big Jack with Bat's help, and Joe would confirm his identity.

"Once we have them in custody, we'll decide what to do with all of them," Jesse said.

Joe knew that Jesse already knew what he was going to do with Big Jack. All this would take place around 3:00 a.m., which would give them a few hours before sun-up. Everyone was armed accordingly, and they managed to round up some dynamite for emergency's sake. Joe had his father's Derringer pistol and a mouthful of angst as his arsenal. He bore his faith in God, his brother's memory, and the love for his family as his armor.

The moon was full on a clear, windy Saturday night in Tucson, Arizona. The conditions were favorable for the attack, as Frank had remarked. The James boys' intelligence proved to be right. Most of Big Jack's men were in town that night and would not be coming back to the ranch. They would likely not be able to move until noon, at that. Joe's heart was pounding just like it was when they were captured by the North Army. Aside from all that had happened to him over the last few years, he was just not suited for this kind of work. He stole a glance at O-B, who smiled at him and knew what he was thinking. O-B shot him a wink, and for a minute, Joe felt better. He and O-B had been through a lot together, and Joe was glad to be with him. As they were finalizing the plans and getting the last details sorted out, Joe thought they all must have heard his heart beating. The wind was making its own noise. The dog would be first.

The men dismounted their horses about three quarters of a mile down the road from Big Jack's ranch. They crept up slowly and surrounded the bunkhouse. There was no activity to be heard. The remnants of Big Jack's men were sound asleep. The Indian snuck up to the house and entered the front porch. They heard a slight whimper, and soon after, the Indian came out with the immense dog draped around his shoulders. The carcass landed on the ground with a resounding thud. The gang and O-B entered the bunkhouse on Frank's signal. Shortly after, O-B peeked his head out and gave Jesse the thumbs-up. All was quiet in the bunkhouse. Joe's blood was racing through his body. The adrenaline high was making him light-headed, and he felt like blacking out, but somehow he was in control. This was the kind of thing that Frank, Jesse, and the rest of the gang encountered on a regular basis—and thrived on. Joe, however, was struggling to maintain.

Jesse, Frank, Joe, Bat, O-B, and the Indian entered the ranch house. Everyone was sleeping, and they were able to get the drop on the entire household. There was Big Jack, his wife, his eighteen-year-old son, and three servants. The Indian and O-B worked quickly to hog-tie and gag the servants. They did not make a sound as they awoke to Frank's shotgun barrel pointed at their faces. Big Jack also awoke to a gun in his face—it was Bat's trusty colt .45.

Jesse immediately started tying him up, as Joe gently bound and gagged his wife. The Indian took care of the boy in the same manner. Joe noticed the look of fear in Big Jack's wife's eyes, and she pleaded with her look, but Joe knew she was going to be okay, so he turned away. The entire operation took less than three minutes. Joe was impressed—no casualties save the dog. Suddenly a door popped open, and a man with his pants barely on busted in. Instantly, he had two shotguns and a colt .45 in his face. He was bound and gagged by Frank while the others looked at each other, trying to figure out who this man was. Big Jack was ungagged, and he let the gang know that this was his brother Bill. Jack recognized Joe's face and let out a laugh.

"How's your brother doing?" he said with an icy smirk. Jesse slammed the butt of his shotgun into the back of Big Jack's head, and he was silenced again.

Frank ordered everyone to check gags and bindings and headed outside. The entire operation took thirtyfive minutes, start to finish. The sun was starting to show is the East horizon, but it would be well past noon before anyone would know what had happened. Everyone but Big Jack and Bill were left behind. Jack's wife struggled and moaned for them to stop, but Jesse just smiled at her and said, "You knew what you were getting into, sweetheart."

They completed the kidnapping with a six-hour head start. The James Gang and the Indian rode out North; and Jim, O-B, and Bat went directly east. They would meet up at the rendezvous point in Las Cruces, New Mexico, in a day and a half.

The James Gang rode north for a few miles and then headed east toward New Mexico. They stopped at nightfall and made camp in the desert. The ungagged their prisoners, and they immediately started asking questions. Frank told them about JJ's and the brothers. He mentioned that Joe wanted them to stand trial in Wisconsin for ordering the murder of his brother. The Wallichs instantly knew why they were there. Jack started in on how Joe and Jim were "rebel scum" and didn't deserve to live.

Jesse stepped up and introduced himself. "Jesse James at your service," he said with a sheepish grin.

At that moment, Big Jack and Bill knew they would never make it to Wisconsin to stand trial. He spat on the ground and cursed the South. Jesse just laughed in his face and said, "Don't think the desert floor is gonna care much."

Frank and Jesse hated the North as much as the Wallich brothers hated the South. That night, without so much as the crack of a twig or the screech of a hawk, their day of reckoning was upon them. The James brothers wasted no time. They told the Wallichs where their loyalties were, pulled up to a strong hanging tree, and proceeded to do what they have done so many times before in hanging the Wallich brothers.

The James Gang met up at the rendezvous point with the rest of the Dundee posse. Joe instantly realized they were not with the company of Big Jack and his brother. Jesse stopped him before he had a chance to say anything. "Me and Frank, we got many vendettas to fill—this was just one of them."

Joe knew what had happened. He felt neither guilty nor vindicated. Jesse understood and clapped him on the shoulder. "Look, son, this was not your doing at all. This was something the James Gang took on all their own."

Joe did not ask any more questions about Big Jack's ranch. The less he knew, the better off he was. They traded their horses for two coaches and made their way back to the midwest, incognito.

The James brothers and some of their gang got off at their home in Missouri. Joe thanked Jesse and Frank for everything they had done for him.

"You'll see us very soon," Jesse remarked.

Joe was not so sure of this, but nodded in agreement. They bade farewell, and the carriage rode off into the dusty night. Joe realized the James brothers risked their lives for him, and he was thankful for them. He was mostly thankful he did not have to witness the hangings, but it was nice to have two fellows like Frank and Jesse James on his side. The war may be coming to a close, but you could not tell them that. They were going to fight until the end, whatever end that might be. Joe thought he had distanced himself from the war as much as he could, but it continued to follow him around like a hungry puppy.

There's just no getting away from it, he thought. With that, he fell into a deep sleep. After nine days of heart-pounding excitement, Joe's body had finally given in. His mind fell into a trancelike calm that would not let go until they arrived in Lacrosse, Wisconsin, three days later.

They took a break from the ride home and decided to stay overnight in Lacrosse at an inn on the Mississippi river. The fall leaves were starting to turn, and the view was spectacular. The gang unpacked and set up for the night in their rooms. Joe was extremely relaxed and was genuinely amazed at how good he felt, considering all he had just been through. They all met in the restaurant for dinner. The inn had a fancy quality while being elegant at the same time. The tables were dressed in red linen, and all of them had a silver candelabra with red beeswax candles freshly lit. The interior of the restaurant was mostly lightly stained cherry wood with a pine floor. There was row of windows facing the river, and the sun was just cresting the trees as the gang sat down for dinner.

"Breathtaking, isn't it?" said a voice from behind Joe.

They turned to look, and their hostess was standing behind them. Joe was immediately caught in her gaze, and as he peered into her soft green eyes, he managed to mutter, "Yes . . . yes, it is."

She smiled at him, as well as everyone else in the group, but he only witnessed hers.

She was a very cute, petite brunette by everyone else's standards, but Joe thought he was looking at an angel. He stared at her so long it made her giggle, which finally broke his trance. "My name is Gina. How are you all doing this evening?" she said in a voice that made Joe melt.

"Hi," he said, again getting lost in her eyes. O-B nudged him with his elbow, and he managed to come back down to Earth. Everyone in the gang had a nice laugh over it.

Gina gathered menus and led them to their table, but she kept glancing at the sheepish boy who refused to take his eyes off of her. Joe did not know what had come over him. He had been with plenty of women, but she was different. There was something about her that he felt he needed to be near, and without knowing why, it was somewhat confusing for him. He kept looking at her while she was seating the other tables. O-B and Bat were somewhat confused at first, but it made perfect sense. Joe always had his brother, and then it was JJ's after Jim had moved on. He needed something to fill the void, and with everything else that was going on, that void was filled with anger and contempt. Now that things were resolved, he was an open book, and it might not be a stretch for Gina to write her own chapter.

When they were finished with dinner, O-B, Bat, Ox, and the Indian all did their part to get Joe to stay at the bar while they all retired to their rooms. Joe was nervous to talk to Gina, but she was intrigued by him and felt comfortable in his eyes. As soon as her shift was over, she joined him at the bar. He was facing the bar and looking down into his drink when she put her hand on his shoulder. He knew it was her, and it instantly put him at ease. He figured out what it was that was special about her in that moment. She made him feel comfortable. He felt like he was back home in Sumner sitting on the porch with Jim pitching stones into the big tin can—only he was thousands of miles away and in a place he had never been before. They talked for hours and then went for a walk along the riverside as the moon lit the way.

Gina's family lived nearby in Minneapolis. She had moved to Lacrosse after she had a run-in with a lawman who had tried to force her to marry him. Her family was sad, but they felt it was for the best, and they visited her often. She had an aunt and uncle who lived a few miles out of town on a farm, and she helped out there as well as at the inn. She was a natural hostess. She was extremely pleasant and had a way of making the customers forget about their bad service or cold meat. She was indispensable according to her manager, who introduced himself a few times after finding out Joe was the owner of JJ's in Dundee. She was astounded with his tales and thought he was completely lying until he pulled out his wad of cash to pay his bar tab. He left ten dollars for the bartender, which was more money than she made in a whole week. Joe being well-off did not hurt his image with his lovely companion.

He got her a carriage ride home, and she made him promise to stay another night at the inn. He went back to the hotel and slept for ten hours, waking up shortly before noon. He went down to have lunch and found that the gang had already left with no trace, except for a note from O-B which read, "Boss, see you next week.PS: two weeks is fine too. The gang."

Joe was glad they understood, but he had always been the understanding one, which made this gesture seem so important to him. He thought of Jim for a second and knew that he was looking down with a smile at him.

That day, he met Gina in a nearby park before her shift started, and they held hands and talked the entire time. She spent the night with him at the hotel, and it was the best time he ever knew. The entire week went by like a whirlwind. They laughed, drank, and danced like they were in a Shakespeare sonnet. They were having dinner Saturday night when Joe decided to take it to the next level.

"Come with me to Dundee," he said as he was holding her hand across the table.

She looked in his wounded eyes and felt tepid about her response. "I can't," she said, "my life is here."

"It's not far, you can come back anytime," he said.

"It's not that, Joe. I'm happy here," she said and pursed her lips as she was fighting the urge to say yes.

"You can be happy with me, you'll have a job there, and we can leave anytime you want," he said, pleading with his eyes.

"I don't know, Joe, it's all a little too soon. I need some time to think about it—let's not ruin this night," she said and smiled at him genuinely. He smiled back at her and nodded.

They finished the night walking along the river with Joe telling her stories of Tennessee and the swim hole he and his brother were so fond of.

"I wish I had one of those," she said.

He laughed, and they walked arm in arm as she leaned her head on his shoulder. They walked on, and everything in the scene was so visible to him. The trees, the stars, the moon—all of it was so present in his senses. He felt as if he would never forget them. He did not notice, however, the dark figure that was following them along the riverbank.

They turned back toward the inn and were nearly there when the figure jumped out of the shadows. Gina gasped for air, and Joe instantly jumped in front of her. The figure was in the shadows, but Joe could see he was pointing a pistol at him.

"What do you want?" Joe asked in as rough of a tone as he had. The figure was still creeping toward them slowly.

In a gruff, terribly low voice, the figure said, "Just what's coming to me, boy'.'

"Who are you?" Joe demanded.

"Never you mind, you Southern trash," the figure blurted out. Finally, the figure crept out into the moonlight. Joe immediately saw the crest on his jacket. It was the familiar ranch brand of Big Jack Wallich—come to haunt him at last.

"Get down on your knees!" the figure demanded.

Joe noticed something familiar about the man. He looked like Big Jack, only smaller. He must have been related, and that only made Joe feel worse. Gina gripped him with her own fear, and he felt her knees weakening.

"Let her go," Joe demanded.

"No such thing," the figure said. "There won't be any witnesses." Joe felt the world he thought he left behind come rushing back. He hated that he somehow managed to bring Gina into it.

"You killed my brother in cold blood—I know you did," the figure said and thrust his pistol into Joe's face. Gina screamed.

The figure pointed his gun at Gina and said, "You better shut your mouth, you little hussie, or you're gonna get it first!"

Joe said, "I didn't do anything to your brother—who are you?"

The figure said, "Don't play stupid with me . . . you gotta know who I am by now."

Joe just looked at his attacker in silence, afraid to give himself away. "Now get down on your knees," the man said.

Joe obliged reluctantly, but Gina was too afraid.

"I said get down!" the man screamed, and he pistol-whipped Gina across the face.

Joe screamed "No!" And he caught her as she fell. She was out cold, and he laid her on the ground softly. "Yeah, that's right boy, you get your last feel in before you die," the man said.

Joe wasn't even paying attention; he was just thinking about Gina and how he felt about her. He wanted to grab her and run as far away as he could. He wanted to go back to Sumner.

He looked up at the man who was about to kill him. He felt anger creep in and fill up his mind with thoughts of rage. He never meant for any of this to happen. He was a good man and had always treated people with respect, but the war and people's hatred of the South surrounded him wherever he went. He didn't deserve any of this. He didn't deserve to have his brother taken away from him so awfully. He was prepared to let Jim go, but not that way. He thought of what his father had told him, right before he left.

"You keep a low profile," he said.

Joe thought of what the meant to him and how he had done his best to stay out of trouble and out of the spotlight. He also remembered what his Uncle Steve had told him once. He said, "Sometimes words that you live by can be words that save your life."

The man standing over him muttered, "Say good-bye to your little hussie." And he pointed the gun at Joe's head. Joe hadn't been paying attention to his hand, but it was in his front pocket, and suddenly he felt his hand on his father's Derringer pistol, which had never been fired since he had it. He gripped the stock. Suddenly, he dropped to the ground, and he heard the man's revolver discharge just as he hit the dirt. In one swift move, Joe pulled the Derringer out of his pocket, and before the man could get a bead on him, he fired it upward and toward the man's general area. He saw the man stagger and fall, his head landing right in front of Joe. He heard the blood leaking out of his head, and he knew that the man was dead. Joe reached over for his newly found friend, who was still lying motionless on the ground.

Joe got off the train in Dundee to an empty platform. He placed his things on the deck and stretched his arms. He took in a bit of the North Woods air and felt glad to be back. He turned to the door of the train and reached inside. A hand clasped his, and it was the most beautiful hand he had ever seen. Gina stepped off the train and gave him a big hug.

"I'm nervous," she said.

"I find that hard to believe," Joe said with a smirk. Gina laughed, and they walked off, arm in arm, as the train steward carried their bags. They walked around the comer and down Main Street. Gina told Joe that she liked Dundee, and that she might be happy here.

"Wait until you see the house!" Joe said to her as he looked into her eyes. He walked with her locked in her gaze for some time. He only stopped when she spotted something that made her gasp.

"Oh my god, look, one of the buildings has been burned down!" she exclaimed.

Joe turned to look and saw JJ's Place, blackened and hollow.

He stood there for a moment and took it all in.

Gina asked, "What is it?"

Joe simply shook his head.

Finally, Chris spotted him from the comer and came over. "I'm sorry, Joe, some of Big Jack's boys came around right after you guys left and torched the place. I managed to get two of them in custody," Chris said. "They are still locked up, but I think Bat is going to take care of this one."

Joe nodded. He looked over at Gina and saw that she had figured out what had happened. "Oh, Joe, I'm so sorry," she said as she looked up at him with her huge soft-green eyes.

He looked down and smiled at her. "Don't be sorry, babe," he said. "I got all I could ever want." And he put his arm around her. She laid her head on his arm.

After telling Bat and Steve about what had happened in Lacrosse, they surmised that the last of Big Jack's gang was wiped out. The brother was John. He was the youngest and the most notorious.

"He ran into the wrong McSweeney," Steve belted out with a chuckle.

They were all pleased to see that Gina was with Joe, and they made her feel as comfortable as they could. The couple spent some days in Joe's house with the gang coming by every now and then to hang out and talk.

Bat had begun rebuilding JJ's, and everyone was pitching in on the job—except Joe. No one thought anything of it though. Neither did Joe. Shortly after he found out about the place being burned down, he decided it was time for him to go. He asked Gina to come with him to Sumner, and though she was still a little unsure, she agreed. She was in love with him, and after the incident in Lacrosse, she was hooked. Her strong sense of being able to take care of someone in need overwhelmed her when it came to Joe. The funny part was that Joe was always the one taking care of everyone else. He never realized how bad he needed that until Gina was there. Now he couldn't imagine living without that—without her.

He wanted to ask Gina to marry him, but he felt it might be a little too soon. He hoped she would like Sumner. She made him agree to make regular trips up there, and he was more than willing to do that. With Bat and O-B staying behind, and Uncle Steve staying in Kenosha, he knew he would miss them far too much to stay away.

On a dusty, cool Sunday in October, they boarded a train for Tennessee. Bat, O-B, Ox, Chris, the Indian, the girls, the entire staff of JJ's—and even Uncle Steve—came down to the station to send them off. It was hard for Joe to say that many good-byes, but he knew he would be back soon enough. As the train rolled out of the station, Joe could only shake his head. It seemed like only yesterday that he, Jim, and O-B arrived in Dundee with wide eyes and empty pockets. So much had changed. He had changed too.

The train ride seemed to go by quickly. The two young lovers were content in each other's arms. Along the ride, Joe noticed every now and then what the war had done to the land. He occasionally saw smoking towns and trampled fields, dead livestock, and burned-out farmhouses. He wondered if the country would ever recover from the war. It had ravaged so much of the land, as well as the people. He thought of Camp Douglas and hoped that they would shut that place down, but with the South having lost the war, he had little doubt the place would continue to scar and even kill its occupants for a long time.

Suddenly and without warning, the train screeched to a halt. "What's going on?" Gina said, surprised and wide-eyed.

"I don't know, stay put," Joe said. He got up and put his hand in his coat pocket. He heard doors opening and shutting and some voices in the car in front of his. He tried to peer through the porthole, but there was a body blocking the other side. The door swung open with a bang, and there he was, standing in front of Joe, with the biggest smirk on his face is that Joe had ever seen—Jesse James himself, followed by Frank. "Hello, Joe! You didn't think you were going to get away from us so easily, did you?"

Joe laughed and shook the hands of his outlaw friends.

"You must be the lovely Gina," Jesse said as he reached out for her hand to kiss. "Frank and I just wanted to say congratulations, and I have a little present for my friend, Joe," Jesse said out loud for everyone to hear. Jesse reached into his pocket and pulled out a velvet case. He gave it to Joe and asked him to open it.

Inside was a pocket watch, handcrafted with an inlay of gold in the face that said, "JJ's Place." On the back was the inscription, "For a friend who should have never given me the time of day. Jesse."

"Thank you, sir," Joe said and shook Jesse's hand again.

Jesse smiled at him and turned to the passengers of the train. "Your trip will not be delayed any longer, folks!" And with that, Jesse and Frank walked off the train. Everyone was looking at Joe, wondering what to think. Joe just turned around and said, "Pranksters—that's all they are is pranksters."

None of them had a clue what had just happened, and as far as Joe was concerned, that was how it would stay. Gina looked at him with a quizzical look, and Joe just smiled at her and said, "Don't worry about it, I'll tell you later."

They stepped out of the train in Memphis, and the McSweeneys were all there to greet him. The introduction of Gina was a welcome one, and they greeted her with open arms. Gina was astonished how well they treated her and wasn't sure what to think. Joe knew she would like it there, and the carriage ride to Sumner cemented that idea for him. The scenery was not nearly as pleasant. The land was scarred in all directions. Ma McSweeney noticed the look on her son's face and knew what he was thinking.

"Don't worry, son," she said. "the war has not touched the McSweeney's land."

Joe smiled at her and was silent for a second. "It may not have touched the land, Mom, but it touched the family—in many ways."

The End

About the Author

Steve Nelson was born in Milwaukee WI. Graduated from Bay View High School. An Army Veteran. After the military, he kicked around a few jobs including bonded courier, home insulator, to truck driver. Before entering the tavern/restaurant business after 20 plus years he retired in 2003 from Nellie's in Bay View, WI. Nellie's was featured in a movie Milwaukee, MN. Steve now lives in Greenfield, WI with his wife, Martina, his son, Joseph, and his Labrador Nellie who has an attitude.

Lightning Source UK Ltd.
Milton Keynes UK
UKHW021605101022
410237UK00013B/2186